Pandanus Online Publications, found at the Pandanus Books
web site, presents additional material relating to this book.

www.pandanusbooks.com.au

Between the Battles

Between the Battles

A NOVEL

HELEN NOLAN

PANDANUS BOOKS
Research School of Pacific and Asian Studies
THE AUSTRALIAN NATIONAL UNIVERSITY

Typeset in Garamond and printed by Pirion, Canberra

National Library of Australia Cataloguing-in-Publication entry

Nolan, Helen.

      Between the battles : a novel.

      ISBN 1 74076 125 1.

      1. Vietnamese Conflict, 1961–1975 — Fiction. I. Title.

A823.4

Editorial inquiries please contact Pandanus Books on 02 6125 4910

www.pandanusbooks.com.au

Published by Pandanus Books, Research School of Pacific and Asian Studies,
The Australian National University, Canberra ACT 0200 Australia

Pandanus Books are distributed by UNIREPS, University of New South Wales,
Sydney NSW 2052 Telephone 02 9664 0999 Fax 02 9664 5420

Production: Ian Templeman, Duncan Beard, Emily Brissenden

to my daughter, Kay
and Major Jim Fritz

Author's Note

Faced with the sudden death of my mother in 1978, and with my then two-year-old daughter not yet able to understand what I had to tell her, I wrote this novel to record a non-combatant's account of the Vietnam War. While many of the events depicted in this book happened — although not always to me — the story itself is fictional. I hope that reading my novel of the Vietnam War enlightens you about what goes on in a war zone during the long hours between battles.

Acknowledgements

This book is dedicated to my daughter Kay, whose very existence provided me with the reason to write it. And to my favourite Green Beret, Major Jim Fritz, because I promised him one evening in Saigon in 1969 that I would one day tell how it felt to be a young girl in a war.

I would like to thank Gwen Maas, who sent me off to war with the words 'Don't worry about anything; the Americans will look after you'. I also thank my dear hootch-mate Kay Woelffing after whom I named my daughter and with whom I shared many red alerts at Cam Ranh Bay, and who gave me the courage to send this manuscript to the publisher. I also acknowledge the work and assistance of my wonderful secretary Janet Gunn, who typed the manuscript. Without their help, faith and constant nagging, this book would still be lying at the bottom of my foot-locker.

Acknowledgement and thanks is also given to Brad Cooper, Manny Palma, Nilda Salvani, Judi Neil, Wendy Andrew, Peggy Annabel, Janice Benco, Carolyn Hatfield, Lessli Strong and Valerie Heath, for encouragement and support.

Above all, I acknowledge the contribution of my war buddies, Anne Barber, Melba Oki and Jill Irish.

Chapter One

RED DOGS, BLACK CATS AND WHITE MICE

SAIGON WAS HOT! Filthy, smelly, white-light, pressing-in-on-you hot. I hadn't been in the country five minutes before I was howling with frustration, wanting to climb back through the cow bails of the immigration section of Tan San Nhut Airport, back into that safe Pan Am world where everyone was polite and nice to me.

I had been hired in Sydney by the United States Department of Defence. They had put a rather innocuous advertisement in the *Sydney Morning Herald* newspaper, which I had answered by post and promptly forgotten. Some months later I received a letter informing me that I had an appointment at the Australia Hotel with a Mr Ricky B. Mansing III, the personnel officer for the Vietnam Regional Exchange. I attended the appointment and gave my name at the reception desk. After a short wait, a small, good-looking man came forward to greet me, shook my hand and escorted me to his suite on the fourth floor. I sat where he indicated. He said, 'Would you like a drink?' I said, 'Yes please', and an hour and several drinks later his next appointment arrived. He indicated that the interview was over, so I left. We had not gone beyond the small talk stage, and the only discussion that in any way related to my purpose for being there was when he had asked me which job I was after in Vietnam, and I had said, 'Typist or anything like that I suppose'.

About three months later, I received a cable: 'YOUR SERVICES URGENTLY REQUIRED STOP PAN AM HOLDS TICKET STOP MANSING VRE.'

I should have been suspicious at this stage, bearing in mind the unorthodox way things had been handled to date, but I was just so excited at the prospect of adventure on high pay that I packed a bag, had 27 shots in two weeks, and flew to Singapore by Qantas 707 before I could have second thoughts.

Now I had arrived, after a stopover in Singapore, and, on reflection, as I stood unhappily searching faces in the crowd in that hot, noisy airport building, I wished I had checked things out from Sydney first. The airport crowd did not seem friendly. Everyone was staring at me. I started to tremble. Then I realised what felt so wrong … I was the *only girl in the airport*. I looked around wildly, starting to panic. All I could see were men, wall-to-wall. Korean soldiers, American soldiers, Thai soldiers, Filipino soldiers, Vietnamese soldiers, and a few Vietnamese in black silk pyjamas, one of whom came forward grinning through stained teeth and grabbed my bag. I was near hysteria. I had cabled my time of arrival to Mr Mansing, but no one had come forward to claim me. I cried aloud to the crowd in desperation, 'Isn't there anyone here looking for me?'

An American soldier, with full dramatics, fell to one knee in a Rhett Butler position and shouted back, 'Honey, Ah've been lookin' for you all ma life.'

The tension was broken. The soldiers nearby all laughed uproariously, and I burst into tears. Within minutes, they became my self-appointed champions; they rounded up a jeep and driver, tipped the Vietnamese *papasan* for my piece of luggage and sent me on my way through the streets of Saigon into Cholon, the Chinese sector, where the head office of the Vietnam Regional Exchange (VRE) and, hopefully, Mr Mansing the Third, were located.

On the drive across town, while I chatted to the driver, I thought about the soldiers at the airport. They had told me they were on their way home after 12 months in the country, and that during that time they would have seen approximately half a dozen white girls. The reason the entire airport crowd was staring at me was that, apart from the fact that a white girl was rare, to see one arrive in the country voluntarily was a shock. They had been dumbfounded.

I still don't know whether to class my arrival date as luck or gross mismanagement. I arrived at the doors of my new workplace at 4pm on New Year's Eve 1967. The soldier in my borrowed jeep carried my bag to the door, threw it inside, pushed me after it and rushed back to his jeep. Before

I could say thank you, he had driven off. I felt I had lost my only friend in the world.

People were hustling in and out of doors off a corridor. It was like a rabbit warren inside. As I was standing there, four girls came out of a door together, chatting, and stopped short when they saw me.

'Yahoo, another round eye,' one shouted, and they swooped on me. 'Kerry, grab her bag. Lil, race out front and see if the Black Cat bus has arrived. Hi, I'm Penny Jones, I'm another Aussie and you must be Holly. We've been waiting all day for you to arrive.'

'Bus is here,' the girl named Lil came running in. The girls pushed me ahead onto a military bus with bold hand painted letters reading 'Black Cat Bus' written down its sides.

'Hey, hey,' I protested. 'Shouldn't I sign in or something?'

'Hell no,' said Penny. 'In-processing takes a whole day, and nothing can be done about you till the second of January at least, so you're coming with us for the holidays.'

The girls tumbled over each other to tell me about Vietnam, the war, the parties, the politics, their jobs. They introduced me to some other girls on the bus from the American Embassy and other US agencies around town, then settled down to talk about their favourite subject — men. Apparently, because ladies were in short supply, we were classified as Precious Cargo, and were treated as such by the American soldiers. Gradually, I was able to sort some sense out of what these girls were telling me all at once.

Penny was an Australian and had been the first Aussie girl to arrive in the country, a week before Lilian. Penny worked in Retail Branch, sorting out inventories, and Lil worked in Personnel and was the one who would in-process me.

Kerry Schwartz was an American, from the mountains of Cheyanne, Wyoming. Both her parents were working in Saigon. Kerry had discovered that holidays in the States were no fun, as all the eligible young men were in Vietnam, so she had decided to join her parents for a vacation.

'It's funny,' she said, 'but back home there are anti-war posters that show a soldier silhouetted against a fabulous sunset and the caption reads "Visit beautiful Vietnam ... fun capital of the world." Silly asses don't realise that they are right.' She grinned at me. 'I hope you're not adverse to parties every night.'

The fourth girl in our group was Chantou, a Chinese who had lived in Vietnam most of her life. She was terrific fun, very droll, and was the translator in moments of difficulty when the girls were out on the town and were harassed by the White Mice. The girls babbled on, talking over each other. I made a mental note to ask about these white mice later.

Our bus arrived at the airport and the young driver explained our way through the checkpoint. Instead of heading towards the part of the airport where I had arrived just a few hours earlier, we turned left and drove for several miles around the perimeter, past camps of soldiers behind barbed wire who waved and shouted to us. One was walking naked from the shower, so we all hung out of the bus windows and whistled and hooted. He hit the dirt! I was impressed with his quick reflexes.

A few miles further on, we came to a grassy area about the size of a football field, hidden from the main airstrip by trees and scrub. The bus pulled over to the edge and we waited. Soon I heard an approaching helicopter and, over the trees and down onto the grass, came a Chinook, the largest helicopter I had ever seen.

The rear door of the chopper opened to form a ramp; the driver started up the bus and drove slowly and carefully into the chopper. The ramp closed up again and we took off. It was dark inside and it took a few minutes for my eyes, and mind, to get used to the dim light.

'We can get off the bus now,' Kerry shouted into my ear. We climbed down, assisted by nice-looking airmen wearing steel helmets and with M16 rifles slung over their shoulders. The noise inside the helicopter was deafening, so I was introduced by signs and mouthings to various airmen. They all kissed me hello. One fellow, Danny, took me by the hand over to the window where I looked down at the countryside.

It was just becoming dusk outside and the scene was beautiful. The forest below was thick and green, with no sign of war anywhere. I had expected the countryside to be devastated, but it certainly wasn't here.

Little clearings with temples set in the centre, rice fields, boys riding buffalo home, clusters of houses with smoke rising from the chimneys — all glowed in the sunset between the dark long shadows. It was a peaceful, rural scene, touched by gold. Little red fireflies bounced around the window in front of me. Danny grabbed me and flung me violently down the length of the fuselage, shouting something I could not hear. He swung the machine gun that rested on a bar at the open door, and started firing at the ground. The Chinook rose steeply. My idyllic sightseeing was over. The fireflies, so pretty, had been tracer bullets. Someone down there was shooting at us!

Heart pounding, I hit the dirt dramatically, as I had seen the soldier do on the way to the chopper pick-up, and as I had seen countless soldiers do in movies. Penny kicked my side with her foot and I turned my head from the floor of the chopper and realised that everyone else was standing upright, pressed against the side of the bus right in the middle of the floor. She indicated by sign language that I was making myself a bloody good full-length target to shots coming from underneath us, and I nodded my understanding sheepishly. I was going to have to listen hard and learn fast, I realised, if I was to survive here for 12 months.

We came on Phu Loi, our destination, just as the sun set. We climbed back onto the bus, which backed off the Chinook on to the helipad, and we waved goodbye to the soldiers who had flown us up from Saigon, never having been able to talk to them properly because of the noise. Kerry said, 'Don't worry, they'll be at the Red Dog party.' As the bus drove off across the airfield towards the main camp, I poured questions out at the girls.

'Hey, one at a time,' they laughed.

Lilian answered me. 'We are now at the headquarters of the 12th Combat Aviation Division, known as the Red Dogs Division. We are invited to their New Year's Eve party and, in all probability, will be the only girls there and will be treated like royalty. We are being billeted with the Black Cats, the 11th Battalion, who are all great guys. They supply us with this bus in Saigon whenever we are stuck for transport. They just stick it on the Chinook and send it down to us. All we have to do is phone Virgil, the adjutant. To make it official, they always send the chaplain down with it, but he's a great guy too. We call him "the bald-headed man in the green suit" for fun.'

We were driving past a well-lit oasis, and I stared in amazement. Palm trees surrounded an olympic-sized blue pool, deck chairs and umbrellas were interspersed between the trees.

'Wow,' I said, 'This is war?'

'Oh these guys have it all right,' Kerry told me. 'They were the first combat division sent into Vietnam by the US Government and they've had time to get themselves organised. That's why we go to their parties in preference to other battalion parties. The food's better, they have learnt to "requisition" things better than the others, and they always hire a good band.'

'And what are white mice?' I asked, remembering.

Chantou answered. 'They are the *Cahn Sat*. The Vietnamese local police,' she said. 'They are full of piss and wind, our version of the SS of Nazi Germany, only, really, they are harmless. They dress in white, so we call them White Mice. Suits them!'

The bus pulled up in front of a row of wooden huts, called hootches, and we alighted to be greeted by a mob of men waving drinks and throwing streamers at us. Kerry, Penny, Lil and Chantou seemed to know everyone, and Kerry shouted above the racket, 'Hey everybody, we've brought you all a new girl.' A cheer went up and people started pressing forward to say hello and offer friendship, but Penny grabbed my arm and hustled me into a nearby hootch.

'We'll shower and change first,' she told me. 'We always dress up for the guys, you know, try really hard to look beautiful for them. Long dresses, jewellery, the works.'

I looked about the room. Bunks lined the walls; I counted eight. A few armchairs were about the room. Coffee tables and magazines, grey metal wardrobes and homemade bookshelves made the room look somehow cosy. Through a door at the back was a step-down concrete-floored area containing a urinal and shower. 'Main toilet is down the end of this row of hootches,' said Penny, seeing my eyes searching.

We took turns to shower and I didn't let any of the girls know that this was my very first cold shower. I shivered under the water as, now the sun had set, the night had become quite cold.

'No hot water in Vietnam,' Chantou told me. 'The electrical system won't support it.'

Kerry lent me a long dress and the girls fussed over my hair with hot curling wands and masses of hairspray.

'Well,' said Lil, standing back to admire the result, 'you're ready to make your official Vietnam debut.'

'Yes, I'd say she looks ready to face that hungry wolf-pack outside,' said Penny, laughing.

'Come on, Aussie,' said Kerry, linking her arm through mine. 'Come meet my gorgeous countrymen in full force.'

'And welcome to my war,' said Chantou, quietly, in the background.

Chapter Two

THEY SAY THE FIRST 12 MONTHS ARE THE HARDEST

A WEEK IN-COUNTRY and it felt like a year. I was now an old hat at things that, a mere seven days earlier, had been traumatic and dangerous. Now I could cross a one-way street and know that I also had to check the other direction, as traffic in Saigon was unpredictable. I knew that I could completely disregard all military regulations, such as curfew (10pm) and the ban on patronising certain bars and restaurants. The defiance of death was a daily game; and I was winning. My reflexes were getting really good. I could hit the dirt now without grazing my elbows or knees on the street, and I found myself constantly checking for alternative exits in public places 'just in case'. I really knew I was settling in, however, when I realised I was thoroughly enjoying the war games and the absolute sense of accomplishment obtained from just making a journey from point A to point B through the city in peak hour (a most dangerous time, as Vietcong were wont to throw satchel charges into crowds).

I felt, too, that I had known my workmates all my life. Only rudimentary questions were asked about one's background, such as hometown, age and marital status. No one seemed to want to know any more and, frankly, I did not want to know much about their previous lives either. We all existed *now* and *here*. Friendships were instant and forever binding. Hatred was a wasted emotion; time was too precious for that. If two people didn't click, they simply avoided each other and no comment was made by either one.

I hated Angela on sight. We met in the snack bar at the PX headquarters and, as we were both from Australia, we decided to share a pot of coffee. After the banalities were over, I suddenly found myself in a contest with her. She seemed to feel it was very important that she establish the position of top dog. She aired her knowledge of in-country matters, of people I should or should not be friendly towards, of how I should handle the job. I resented her attitude. It was one of 'I'm right, nothing you have learnt so far is of any use, so listen to me or else you'll be in trouble'. We finished our coffee, said such things as 'Nice meeting you, see you again soon', and disappeared completely from each other's lives. I saw her occasionally around the office halls and we always nodded and smiled, but we both knew that there would be no more social intercourse. Poor Angela, she never got out of Saigon during her whole 12 months tour of duty. She never knew what she missed.

As a result of trial and error, I found myself in a circle of good friends and the camaraderie that developed between us was, I imagine, the type of love and friendship that makes old soldiers today stick to their RSL clubs and march in the Anzac Day parades. We shared everything with each other: clothes, lovers, experiences, grief and joy. We girls *loved* each other in a way that not many women ever experience.

At the Black Cat and Red Dog party on New Year's Eve, those girls took me under their wings and tried to condense their experiences to lessen my confusion. They could see the look on my face when I was confronted with more than 100 sex-starved, slathering men. Kerry said later that she had watched my face go through a kaleidoscope of shock, fear, wonder, amazement and finally relaxation, as I walked out that door of the hootch into the mob. Guys were yelling, 'Who's the new lady? Lemme at her! Get out of the way and let's get a look! Have a beer. Do you wanna bourbon? Where's she from? What's her name?', and all were jumping up and down and trying to get my attention, like puppies on sale in a pet shop.

I was confused and afraid, and hung back behind Penny, who pulled me forward and shouted, 'Hey you guys, shaddup.' Instant silence! I was filled with awe. I had my first taste of the power of a female in that place. All Penny had to do was say the word and they obeyed. 'Her name is Holly,

she's single, she's Australian,' she called, and the crowd then
quietened down and things became relatively normal again.
Wow, I thought. I must remember how to do that.

I was formally introduced to a few fellows standing
close by and then I was escorted to the barbecue area by
about a dozen of my brand new friends. Their accents were
delightful. I had never heard American accents en masse
before, only in the movies, and the variety pleased me.
A Texan, who was typically tall and lanky and who drawled
beautifully, fixed a plate of food for me. A gentleman from
the Deep South, or so he said, with a very soft voice and
eyes, handed me a mint julep 'Made especially for another
deep southerner'. His name was Virgil, and he was the Camp
Adjutant. I liked him very much.

After dinner, during the dancing, to a great Filipino
travelling band hired especially for the occasion, whistles
were blown at various times to indicate certain time zones
that had reached the new year. At 10pm, a whistle was
blown and the cry 'Happy New Year, Australians' went up.
I howled with emotion and found myself being hugged and
hugged again by my compatriots.

As the night wore on, I found myself being
monopolised by Virgil. As he outranked almost all of my
other prospective dance partners, no one was rude enough to
cut in on us. Rank does have its privileges, although at this
early stage I was not aware that rank-pulling was going on. In
the ladies room later on, I asked Penny and Lilian if we were
expected to sleep in the hootch provided for us, as I was

beginning to have other ideas about where I would spend the night. They roared with laughter.

'No way,' they shouted in unison. 'We don't come up here to sleep *alone.*'

All the girls had special fellows, and those who shared rooms with other guys had organised their room-mates to move into other hootches for the night, leaving each one a room with complete privacy. I inquired as to Virgil's arrangements. He had his own quarters, *with hot water.* That settled it. I was his for the night!

'Hey, hey. Don't rush into anything,' warned Penny. 'How short or long is he? We'd better find that out first.'

Vivid pictures flashed through my mind.

'Ohmygod,' I said. 'Is the choice *that* good?'

The girls giggled and exchanged dirty, mischievous looks. 'Shall we tell her or tease her?'

'No,' they took pity on my ignorance. 'Short means not much time left in-country. It's no use getting involved with someone who is short, because you just get fond of each other and he has to go home. Long means he has, say, over six months to go yet. Now, never sleep with someone who's long, because they get possessive and you can't just fade into oblivion in this place when you want to end an affair. It's not worth running a risk with a long guy.'

'My ideal length of fellow,' said Carolyn, an embassy girl who joined us, 'is about three or four months left in-country. Nice enough time to get to know each other really well, time enough for some really good loving but not long enough to get hopelessly involved and hurt.'

I liked the girls' philosophy. I certainly wasn't in
Vietnam to find a permanent man, but I didn't want a
succession of quick affairs either. What the girls were talking
about made sense to me.

'And remember,' warned Kerry, who had come looking
for me, 'everybody in Vietnam will know who you sleep
with, and when, and where. We are the central topic of
conversation in Saigon mess halls and bars, apart from the
actual war which takes up 90 per cent of the men's thoughts.
The other 10 per cent is gossip. So make sure you make each
lover worthwhile. It's impossible to have a secret in this place.'

And so, armed with all this advice, I waited till my
self-appointed lady guardians had found out Virgil's length.
Fifteen minutes later, Penny sidled up to me on the dance
floor and whispered in my ear, 'Seven inches or weeks, take
your pick. Nice!'

Virgil and I left the dance floor together and headed
towards his hootch. I could feel the back of my neck going
scarlet as a hundred pairs of eyes watched. I could almost
hear the sigh rise from the crowd. Envy? Lust? I felt like
running, but just hung onto Virgil's arm and wobbled off into
the night with him.

Back in Saigon, I was able to look a fellow straight in
the eye when he asked me out on a date (which was
approximately every man I was introduced to) and say, 'How
short are you?' without even a glimmer of a smile. And the
question was always taken seriously. No one ever made a rude
joke about it. The answer always came straight and honestly.

But another aspect came up that caused a dilemma. When a fellow was short and I would say sorry, too short, he would say, 'But you're not going to let me go home after 12 whole months in this damn place without a night with a girl who speaks my language, are you?' Or 'I don't want to break down and cry in front of my wife when I get home. Help me through just the next week or so, will you?' Sometimes I relented, sometimes I didn't. It just depended on how good-looking he was. Sometimes *I* was so good that he forgot the wife back home and re-enlisted for a further six months.

I was finding life rather difficult because I was not getting much sleep. We worked 11 hours a day (three hours of it on paid overtime) six days a week, and the after-office hours were spent making up for all the wasted work hours. Upstairs in the office building, which was a converted picture theatre on Petrus Ky in Cholon, was the Choi-oi Bar. *Choi-oi* was the Americanisation of the Vietnamese expression '*Troi-oi*', meaning 'heavens above' or 'good grief' or something similar. There were no swear words in the Vietnamese language, so this came the closest to our rather crass 'Oh hell'. Anyway, the Choi-oi Bar was where Attitude Adjustment Hour began each evening at 6pm sharp. The Attitude Adjustment Hour was also known as the Prayer Meeting. Happy Hour was from 6pm to whenever the bar closed, and the drinks were therefore always half-price. They were nearly always free for the girls. This is where we would arrange to meet a date, if he was calling for us from the office.

If we were meeting our date at home, we would still find time
for a quick drink before going home for the night.

It did not occur to me at the time to question how
such a place as the Choi-oi Club, which was essentially a
private bar, could be so lavishly appointed or how the drinks
could be so cheaply priced without some sort of subsidy.
Later, or course, I knew that it was decorated with black
market goods and money: plush red velvet wallpaper,
expensive carpets, a teak leather-topped bar, all 'requisitioned'
by the heads of the PX in Saigon and diverted for their own
private use. These purchases were authorised by a colonel of
the VRE. The engineer who fitted out the bar, a Canadian
called Don Sale, told me that the cost was $48,000 and it
was charged to the Long Binh and Saigon Depots. The
living quarters of a particular commander were also
decorated with 'requisitioned' goods, total cost $50,000. He
had two bathrooms, three bedrooms, three water pumps
(electrically operated from his own generator), a bar,
carpets, et cetera, all charged to the depot and authorised by
the colonel. Peter Ray, an Australian engineer working for
the PX, also told me that the Korean firm, Bue Huong
Constructions, was paid $61,000 to carpet the commander's
office in the Cholon headquarters building — with carpet
that was already US property!

The Australian work contingent, a small bank of men
and women, often discussed the rip-offs that the top military
and civilian Americans were involved in. We were
absolutely amazed, not only by the dishonesty of the fat-cats,

but by the complete acceptance of what they were doing by other staff members. It was the *done thing* to make as much money and to make oneself as comfortable as possible, at the expense of the US Government. These were the *perks*. We were left open-mouthed at the blatant, 'official' stealing that was done by top personnel. Howard Easton was on the best lurk. The norm in Asian society is to pay for privileges. We call it payola, or bribes, but to the Asian, that is the way you get the job you want. And to hold a concession to the great PX is certainly a big privilege and one worth paying tremendous sums for. Howard gave the lucrative garbage collection concession to his girlfriend, a little Vietnamese girl, who promptly organised her family members as garbage truck drivers to collect the rubbish from the offices and stores all over the Saigon area. Then she lined up the store workers, who, for a fee of course, threw into the garbage pails such items as stereo tape decks, complete with speakers, cartons of beer, soda and cigarettes, shoes, clothing, cameras, hairspray, wristwatches, you name it. The security guards at the PX stores were US enlisted men, who looked the other way when the garbage was carried out in return for the privilege, later in the night, of the company of the female shop assistants. Can it ever be estimated how much American taxpayers' money went out the back door of the stores in this way?

But the deal that made me whistle was the one made by a top American civilian logistics man. A shipload of airconditioners arrived at Saigon Port and, under a heavy veil of secrecy (to prevent theft), they were taken to the rice mill on the outskirts of Saigon for storage. The American then arranged to have the rice mill burgled and the airconditioners removed to his own hiding place. The PX then made a claim through the insurance and claims branch and had the full cost refunded. The American then sold the air-conditioners on the black market for three times their price to Korean, Thai and Filipino troops as well as to American soldiers, who were not willing to wait until the next shipment came in and so were prepared to pay the inflated price. The clever part of his plan was that, as a logistics man, he could prevent or delay the next shipment thus cornering the market. Months later, when the next shipment of airconditioners finally arrived, he did the same thing again. I estimated that he made about $200,000 on each deal. Have you ever heard the one about the airconditioned bunker?

The first shipment of Sealand containers to arrive at Cam Ranh Bay on the mid-coast of Vietnam was doomed. Some American officials had figured that too much stuff was being ripped off through Saigon Port and, to cover things up, they blamed the Vietnamese. They decided that 'sensitive' materials should be sent to Cam Ranh Bay, which was on an island, and which could be completely isolated from the Vietnamese. Off-loading was done by the Seabees onto barges for shipment elsewhere in-country. The first Sealand containers off-loaded held a shipment of whisky. It filled 12 barges, which were then floated down the river towards a trucking depot. Between the wharf and the truck depot, on high water, the barges disappeared. Not just the whisky, mind you, but the barges. I always wondered how much a barge bought on the black market. In fact, who would want a barge, and what on earth could they do with it afterwards? After all, it's not exactly the sort of thing you could take home and say 'Look what I found', is it?

During my induction period, I had been told the dos and don'ts of survival in Saigon. Don't drink the water, don't pat stray dogs, do eat in the recommended restaurants (a pay-off for someone?), don't travel on public transport, do clutch wristwatch and handbag closely while walking on the streets as the Vietnamese were dishonest and would steal me blind, don't bother to learn too much of the language, don't make friends with the local nationals, and so on. It must have been our convict heritage or our supposedly national aversion to authority, but the Australian girls invariably did just the opposite to the American rules. We all drank our tap water and lived. We made ice-blocks from tap water and fed it to our American guests at home as a private joke among ourselves. We never took malaria tablets (they were huge orange once-a-week pills, which produced bodily effects known as the Saigon Quickstep). We made friends with neighbourhood women and children. We had a favourite *papasan*, a kindly toothless old gentleman who waited each morning outside our villa with his pedicab to pedal us to work. We went to his home and met his wife and children. We ate in Vietnamese restaurants, Japanese and Chinese restaurants, and tasted the exotic culinary delights denied the fussy American. Kerry's parents, Phil and Pamela Schwartz, became very native and very involved with local customs and people. Pamela Schwartz became our very own *mamsan*, and mothered us all. She and Phil sought out contact with the local people and made many friends in all strata of social life in Saigon. They were radically different to the usual American civilian in that part of the world, and they opened my eyes to the fallacies of the official American attitude.

I had been issued with a ration card, an identification card and a non-combatant's certificate of identity with my photograph and fingerprints on it. The ration card was a different colour to the one Kerry had and I queried this. Because she was an American, even though she was hired casually in-country, she was allowed to purchase 'luxury' goods from the PX. We Australians were allowed only the basics — soda, beer, a ration of booze each month, six cartons of cigarettes a month, and any other item from the PX store up to $20 in value — with the exception of 'sensitive' and electronic goods. Kerry, on the other hand, could purchase anything from a Ford motor car to a Noritake dinner set, electronic equipment, cameras and, most importantly, she had commissary privileges. We were denied the right to purchase food! We were not even allowed into the commissary. In fact, if we were caught in possession of any restricted goods, even if they were a gift, we were breaking the law. Unfair? Certainly. The Australians had been hired directly by the US Department of Defence and yet we were not entitled to the same protection or privileges as those given to the American employees. We were not allowed to use the APO, the postal system run by the military. We were expected to use the Vietnamese mail service and, as never a week went by without a post office somewhere being bombed, and the fact that very little mail ever got through to Sydney from Saigon, it was pretty useless. We were forced to cheat in order to write home to our anxious families. Thank God for the Australian APO system. Penny and Lil had found some willing Aussie soldiers who sent and received mail for us through their system. Thanks boys.

But the worst thing, and the thing that was heartless and cruel, was prohibiting us from using the commissary. This was run by the US Embassy and only American personnel were allowed into the store. It was like a supermarket. To us, it was like a dream. If we stayed on the straight and narrow in official eyes, we had two choices for stocking our cupboards: we could live on Melba toast, chips, peanuts, canned spaghetti and booze (the approximate range of food sold in PX outlets), or we could buy from the local market dried fish, weevil-riddled rice by the sack, *nuoc mam* (rotten fish) sauce, very expensive but doubtful pork and chicken, or live fish, fowl and pork and slaughter it ourselves. Of course, we set out to con any American who came our way to buy us food from the commissary. There were lean times, but boy, when someone came in our door with a case of steaks, fresh butter and eggs under his arm, anything we had was his.

We were allowed to eat in mess halls, but only as a guest of an American. After a while, the doorman at Five Oceans BOQ (Batchelor Officers' Quarters), which was the BOQ closest to our office, became used to us begging for admittance for a feed and he let us in without much of a scene. Oh, those salads, those jellos, those rotten green frankfurters, even shit-on-a-slate (S.O.S. to them, mincemeat on toast to us), were delicious.

There was a snack bar at work but the food, with the exception of the French toast, was practically inedible and we patronised it only in a dire emergency. One evening as I sat on Colonel Verona's knee in the Choi-oi Club, I complained bitterly to him of my weight loss (from 57kg to 43kg in eight weeks) and, a few nights later, he had a surprise for us. He had 'requisitioned' a freezer, refrigerator and stove, barbecue and tables and chairs, and had turned the outside patio of the club into a dinner area. It was wonderful. From then on, at least three nights a week, we ate at the office with the compliments of Uncle Sam. Other office staff were charged about $1.50 for a meal of steak, lobster tails, salad, chips and champagne. Lovely.

Bit by bit, I organised my life to make it bearable. I had my hair cut really short so I could shampoo the sweat out of it night and morning (in cold water, of course). I found a barber on the sidewalk of Huong Vung Street and sat on his little stool, right there in the middle of the path with people walking around us, while he cut my hair.

I hated my job as a typist in the logistics branch, but I persevered, as I had discovered the Manning Document — a computer-generated list of available jobs — and scanned it eagerly each week for a position to which I could transfer. I felt my job was futile. What was the use of arranging for all these goodies to come into the country for sale in a store to 90 per cent of the US contingent in Vietnam, when the meagre 10 per cent who were doing the fighting rarely got the goodies? Every fighting man was supported by nine back-up personnel. And it was these back-up personnel, or support troops, who were having a ball and making millions of dollars at the fighting man's expense. Oh yes, Saigon was the fun capital of the world.

Weekends were always taken up with a chopper flight to a party somewhere, more often than not at Phu Loi, where we were always made welcome. By weekends, I mean Saturday night and all day Sunday. Every night during the week, we either ate at the Choi-oi Club, had people in to dinner (they always had to bring the food, but we did the entertaining in return), or we managed to line up a party to go to where we made a beeline for the food and stuffed ourselves. Oh, we were a hungry lot.

Chinese New Year, or Tet, was approaching, and we were all called into the commander's office and given our emergency evacuation maps and a nice little historical lecture on the meaning of Tet to the local nationals. The commander told us that the Military Assistance Command (MACV) had advised him that intelligence showed a big

North Vietnamese and Vietcong build up around Saigon, particularly in the Cholon district, and that severe fighting could be expected, possibly in the streets. We were to attempt to come to work each day during the four-day Tet holiday period, unless of course it was too dangerous. I had already made up my mind that it was going to be too dangerous for me. No way was I going to trot along the road to work if there was any excuse to stay home and sleep. We were given the afternoon off the day before Tet to organise our ration supply (ha, ha). I still don't know what the Americans thought we ate. We quickly rounded up a few GIs lurking outside the commissary and, within an hour, had our refrigerator full enough to last for four days. A quick trip to the PX and we bought up our month's ration of booze, soda pop and cigarettes. We were ready.

Lil suggested that we spend our last night of freedom eating out in a well-known Chinese restaurant deep in the heart of Cholon. We all agreed, grabbed our purses and rushed outside to hail a pedicab. Off we went to the Dong Khanh Hotel, which was built in the traditional Chinese style of five floors. On the ground floor were wooden tables with no cloths, rickety chairs and betel-spitting patrons. As the floors went higher so the decor and service became progressively better. We ate on the fifth floor.

I'll never forget that night. It was the best food I have ever eaten, and we were the only white faces in the room and were treated with deference. We were seated at a table on blue velvet-covered chairs, the tablecloth was snowy, and fresh flowers were in a vase in the centre. We had a waiter each. The ceiling was gold mirrors with chandeliers hanging down and, right in the centre of the room close to our table, was a tinkling fountain. We were well into our meal when Penny, choking on a mouthful, suddenly burst out laughing. We looked at her curiously. She squealed, 'look at the fountain!' We all turned. Where there had been four marble cherubs standing peeing decoratively into the pond (hence the tinkling sound), there were now five. A small Chinese boy had climbed onto the fountain wall and had joined his marble mates in a pee. We just didn't know where to look! It is considered terribly rude and uncouth to show any emotion in public in Vietnam and we couldn't lean back and roar with laughter as we desperately wanted to. We had to cover our faces with our napkins, choking, tears streaming down our faces, trying not to look at each other. I turned away from the table, shoulders shaking, trying to suppress my laughter and pull myself together. I looked around the room, but the complete nonchalance of the other diners eating as if nothing unusual was happening, made it worse. I got up and raced to the ladies' room at the other end of the dining room, closely followed by Kerry, Penny and Lil. We pushed open the door and fell inside, hanging onto each other, utterly helpless with laughter.

Eventually, we pulled ourselves together and I took the opportunity to use the toilet. A little boy was sitting on a velvet stool in the corner and, as I approached the cubicle, he got up and rushed over and opened the door for me.

He bowed me into the toilet and then locked the door after me from the outside. I didn't like being locked in. I could hear the laughter starting up again from the girls.

'Let's pay him to leave her in there,' they were giggling.

I wondered if I should flush the toilet, or if the boy might consider that to be his privilege. I knocked politely three times and he opened the door to let me out. He handed me soap and a towel and a plate to put his tip on. Truly, the most royal pee ever.

The bill for the four of us came to just more than $300, the usual Saigon price for a meal. When we stepped outside, it was about 11pm, well after curfew on the night before Tet. The streets were teeming with Chinese and Vietnamese, which was unusual. I realised after a while that this was because all the US military and civilian personnel were indoors tonight, and the locals had their streets to themselves. It must have been a nice feeling for them not to have foreign watchdogs for once. We were trying to hail a pedicab when out of the throng pedalled our very own *papasan*, grinning and showing his gums. As there were four of us, we needed another pedicab, so he co-opted his mate, who was passing by, and we all climbed aboard.

A pedicab is a strange conveyance. It is a two-seater with a wheel at each side and a hood than can be folded back over in case of heat or rain. Behind the seat is a third, much larger wheel on top of which is a bicycle seat. The pedals are on each side of the large rear wheel and the handlebars stick

out each side of the passenger seat. It is a reverse, penny-
farthing-type tricycle with the passenger seat between the
front wheels.

Lil and Penny shared the pedicab with *papasan's* mate,
and Kerry and I shared our old friend's conveyance. *Papasan*
yelled '*di di*' to his mate and pedalled off. His mate pedalled
furiously to catch up. *Papasan* looked behind him and
pedalled even faster. It was a race. They grinned at each
other and yelled challenges. We screamed in excitement,
egging them on. Penny waved a fistful of money at her
papasan, who screeched and pedalled even faster. We waved
money at our driver, who looked like he would have a heart
attack, he was pedalling so hard. More than a little drunk, we
girls made enough noise to wake up the whole of Saigon, but
our backstreet journey home went unobserved, as the streets
were dark and deserted away from the main Cholon area.

At last we arrived home, jaws aching from shouting
and laughing, physically exhausted. Both *papasans* were red
and panting, veins standing out on their foreheads. The
winner was our very own *papasan*, by about half a metre only,
and we gave him $20. He was terribly pleased — I figured he
could probably retire on that princely sum. And, because the
other *papasan* had worked just as hard, we gave him a like
amount. They kept grinning and saying '*Cam on*' which is
thank you, so we invited them into our home and fed them
some good Yankie beer. Hence, we spent the night before
Tet, the night so feared by the Americans, entertaining two
probable Vietcong in our home. We gave them cigarettes

and a sixpack of beer each and waved goodnight to them, calling 'Cam on, cam on' to them in their own language.

Back inside, we flopped down on our beds and rehashed the night's events with much laughter. Penny got up and barricaded the doors and Kerry and I checked the windows to see that all the bars were secure. Lil closed the shutters.

We had had our wild night out. Now we were battened down in our little house in Cholon, waiting to see what tomorrow and Tet 1968 would bring.

Chapter Three

THE 1968 TET OFFENSIVE

I AWOKE AT DAWN. *Mamasan* was already up, her pallet packed tidily away, coffee pot boiling on the little kerosene stove. It smelled good and my throbbing head eased a little at the thought of a strong cup of the brew. Penny, Lil and Kerry were still sound asleep, so I tiptoed around the room collecting my things to have a shower.

Our little villa was a two-storey place or, rather, a large ground floor with an attic room above. *Mamasan* and her daughter, Van, lived upstairs and we four girls shared downstairs. *Mamasan* owned the house. In our section there were double French-style shutter doors leading to the street, across which we slipped a wooden bar each night. There was a back entrance into a side lane, which was an ordinary wooden door to which we had attached a very large bolt on the inside. The living room, being central to the house, had no windows and its side wall was a party wall with the villa next to ours. The only bedroom, which we all shared, was at the front of the house, and opened to a verandah through shuttered French windows. We were situated on a corner and the only room with proper windows was the scullery/shower/toilet room, which faced onto the lane. The windows in this room were glass louvres with bars outside set into the wooden windowsills. We felt secure, but this morning I double-checked the barricades 'just in case'.

Humming to myself, I stepped into the shower room, hissing when the icy water hit me. I hated the cold water and only ever had perfunctory washes. The girls used to joke about how quick I was in the shower. This morning I plunged under the water, lathered up as best I could standing to one side and plunged back under again to rinse off. Standing with my eyes shut I reached for my towel, feeling along the window ledge where the towel rail was. My hand encountered another hand. I shrieked and my eyes flew open. A grinning Vietnamese face was peering through the partly opened louvres. I raced out shouting and quaking. *Mamasan* ran into the scullery and I pointed a shaking finger to the shower room. She went in and I heard her speaking rapidly in her native tongue. She came out and went to the back door, letting the door open a few centimetres only. When she had made sure I was robed, she opened the door and beckoned a White Mouse into the room. He looked around and then stalked through the house, haughtily checking our defences before stalking out again. *Mamasan* gave him some money on his way out.

'What was all that about?' a bleary-eyed Kerry asked, coming into the scullery. 'I woke up and there was a White Mouse in my room.'

Mamasan explained that the local police were doing a door-to-door check of defences, but added that she really thought they were checking on her to see how many people lived in the house for taxation purposes.

Penelope and Lil came in, still in their nighties, and we sat down on stools to have coffee, which *Mamasan* poured for us. 'Happy Tet,' we chorused to her, and gave her silver money for luck. We also gave her and Van little red paper-covered sweets to help her towards prosperity in the New Year. *Mamasan* was delighted with our gifts and said she didn't realise that foreigners knew the customs of her country. She seemed to be really pleased. Van scowled though and muttered something to her mother.

'Aren't you happy today, Van?' Kerry asked.

'No Kelly,' said Van. 'I worried. First person to visit house during Tet is one who makes next year good or not; and our first one was police!'

Van and *Mamasan* invited us upstairs and we climbed up the wooden stairs to their attic room. In the centre of the room was a table on which was a statue of Buddha surrounded by red candles, which *Mamasan* lit solemnly. They had arranged flowers and candles around the statue. Little gifts in paper were also at the feet of the Buddha. The God of the Kitchen was made to feel welcome in his spirit form and *Mamasan* and Van fervently asked for peace and prosperity, food and clothing for the coming year. We sat quietly, entranced by the solemnity of the occasion, and more than a little proud at being asked to witness it.

Downstairs again, we discussed whether we would try
to get to work.

'I think it looks quiet outside,' said Lil, 'but is it TOO
quiet?'

We peered through the kitchen windows; not a soul
was on the street. A few scraggy dogs wandered up the dusty
road, but there was no sign of human life.

The matter was decided for us when a knock on the
door revealed our *papasan*, still grinning from last night's
fracas, indicating that he was ready to pedal two of us to
work. We tossed for the privilege and Kerry and I won.
Dragging *Papasan* inside, we gave him a cigarette and coffee
while we rapidly changed into our shifts and sandals.
Grabbing purses, we went outside and seated ourselves in the
pedicab. *Papasan* leapt on the back and pedalled off around
the corner onto the main street. There were a few American
soldiers at the entrance of the Five Oceans BOQ and they
yelled, 'Hey, get inside you fools', as we went past. Arriving
at the office, we paid *Papasan* and were immediately hustled
indoors by the soldier on guard at the post at the front of the
building. We wandered along the deserted halls till we found
a little group of soldiers in a back room huddled around the
radio. We listened in growing fear. Radio Armed Forces
Vietnam was broadcasting that all civilians and military
should stay indoors; only those on orders elsewhere should
attempt to leave their homes. Damn, I thought, if we had
owned a radio we need not have risked our lives on the
streets that morning. But it was illegal for Australians to own

any electrical item available from the PX store. Kerry had not yet bought one for herself that we could listen to, and, of course, none of us had thought to bring a radio with us from Australia.

Captain Richard, who appeared to be in charge of those in the office that day, sent an enlisted man upstairs to the commander's quarters, which adjoined the Choi-oi Club. He returned shortly with the keys to the commander's big black limousine and he said he would quickly drive us back home. Kerry showed great commonsense in refusing. 'We would be sitting ducks in a big Yank tank this morning,' she argued. 'Let us get home the way we came.'

So we poked our heads outside and, thankfully, *Papasan* was still outside, leaning on his pedicab under a shop awning across the street, sipping on a can of Coke. We whistled to him and he came trotting across. 'Back home *Papasan?*' we begged, and he nodded. By now he too had heard the news that a major enemy force was moving on the city and he knew full well the risk he would run by pedalling two white girls in full view through the streets. Marauding Vietcong would think us an exceptionally good target.

Papasan lifted a finger in a 'stay there just a minute' gesture and went back across the street. He went into the sidewalk café and emerged some minutes later carrying some hessian rice sacks and two coolie hats. We climbed aboard his cyclo and he draped the sacks over our knees like a blanket, placing a coolie hat on each of our heads. Thus garbed, and unable to see what was happening or where we were going, we trusted ourselves to the good god Buddha, the Spirit of the Kitchen, and to *Papasan*. It was a nerve-racking 10-minute ride home, neither of us speaking to each other for fear of being overheard by a passer-by.

Once home, *Papasan* yelled in Vietnamese outside our door, *Mamasan* opened the door and we bolted inside. It all seemed terribly dramatic, like playing cowboys and indians as a child, but we were both shaking and scared. 'Cam on,' we yelled, safe inside, '*cam on, Papasan*, and Happy Tet to you.'

Penny and Lil pressed us for news.

We told them all we knew, Kerry adding that she had phoned her parents' home from the office and her father had told her to bring us all to his home immediately. We thought it was a good idea and I know I would have felt safer there as it was situated in the American Sector, or 'Embassy Row', as it was jokingly called. But how to get there was another matter. We couldn't endanger *Papasan* again, we couldn't run the risk of walking to the main road and trying to flag a taxi, and we couldn't just walk approximately two miles in the present situation.

'Face it, girls, we're stuck here for the duration,' said Kerry mournfully. She knew her parents would be worried sick about us all, so we resolved to make the best of our enforced isolation and ask *Mamasan* and Van to teach us how to play mah-jong.

After that, our first day, which we called New Year's Eve day, passed uneventfully. We learnt mah-jong and a good deal of Vietnamese words from *Mamasan* and Van, mainly by doing funny little drawings of things and writing English under them, to which they would add the equivalent Vietnamese and tell us how to pronounce it. That day I learned to count to 10 in Vietnamese, to say my age of 26 (*hi-moui-sow*, phonetically) of twenty-six, to say 'I am an Australian and I am a Cheap Charlie', which never failed to make Van collapse in a giggling heap, and many other words, such as thank you, scram (*di di*), pork, water, tea, dog, 'I want', and various articles of clothing.

Towards dusk, *Mamasan* and Van went upstairs to change into their finery for the celebration of their New Year's Eve. Van looked beautiful when she reappeared wearing a gold silk *au-dai*, the very sexy Vietnamese national dress, with white satin trousers underneath edged in lace. On her little feet were gold mesh high-heel sandals. *Mamasan* wore an *au-dai* of a rusty brown colour with black satin trousers and red shoes. They had dressed their hair and both looked exotic and beautiful. We wished them a happy evening, settled on a password we could both understand of 'Bloody Aussies' (which we figured could not be deciphered by any Vietnamese other than *Mamasan* and Van) and bolted the door behind them as they left.

'Bring on the drinks,' shouted Lil, suddenly gay. 'Let's celebrate New Year properly.'

About 3am the mortars started hitting the city. They seemed to be coming from the south, going over our roof with long sighing whistles and landing deep in the heart of Saigon.

Penny quickly got up and doused the lights. We sat in the darkness, holding hands. 'I hope their aim is good,' whispered Lil. 'What do you mean?' I whispered back. 'They are probably aiming for American installations, so most of their targets will be in central Saigon,' she answered. We all silently mused on this information.

'Shit!' In the darkness, Penny stood up. 'The bloody main PX store is right NEXT DOOR to us,' she cried. They'll be aiming for it for sure.'

She lit the candle and looked at each one of us. 'We've got to get out of this place,' she announced, 'and pretty soon.'

But how? We discussed waiting till *Mamasan* and Van came home, and borrowing clothes and disguising ourselves to walk to the Schwartz home. The Australian Embassy was miles away, downtown in the Caravelle Hotel. 'Besides,' said Lil, 'they are sure to get hit, so we'd be no safer there.' We bandied alternatives, expanding them and finally rejecting all. We couldn't walk for miles in the dark, mortars whizzing around, and us unable to speak the language. We couldn't get hold of a vehicle to make a mad drive to safety, mainly because none of us knew how to steal a car (I made a mental note to learn how, though).

Finally we decided (like we had a choice) to stay put and hope for the best. So we went to bed after carefully placing our mattresses under the wooden framed beds. I got up halfway through the night and put my mattress back on top of the bed; I felt that it would afford better protection on top of me rather than below me.

It was a long night, punctuated by explosions and gunfire, which seemed to be getting closer as the dawn came. I did not sleep. *Mamasan* and Van did not come home.

In the early light, I went into the scullery and cautiously lifted the louvres to peer out. Two dead dogs lay a few feet from the window. As I watched, a wizened old man scuttled from the house opposite and dragged one dog's body back into his home. I supposed he was going to cook it and eat it. I hoped we would not be reduced to that, at the same time wondering if I should duck out and bring the other body into our home. But the thought of butchering and eating dog made me heave.

I closed the shutter just as it splintered. My hand was badly cut, a triangle of glass slicing into the heel of my left hand. Screeching and holding my wrist, I ran back into the living room. I vowed there and then I would not open the louvres again till all this was over.

Penny bathed my wound and said she thought it needed stitching, so, with a boiled darning needle and thread, and with Lil and Kerry patting and soothing me, Penny inserted four untidy stitches into my hand. Christ, it hurt. I thought I had better have a brandy for breakfast to ease the pain. The girls joined me and, by mid-morning, we were all drunk. We worried aloud about *Mamasan* and Van, our favourite *papasan*, the Schwartz family, all our friends, the boys up at Phu Loi, the 25th Infantry Division, the poor dead dogs in the street, the world political situation and our beloved families back in safe old Sydney Town. We cried on each others' shoulders. We had canned spaghetti for lunch and another two bottles of booze. I must have drunk two entire fifths of bourbon that day, but I never got sick or dizzy, just morbid, rotten drunk.

If the Vietcong had chosen that day to break into our little house, they probably would have been able to shoot us all, we were so drunk. As it was, they tried to get in through the back door the next morning and Penny, with a raging hangover and as cranky as hell, shouted, 'Piss off, *di di*, you bloody little bastards', and they beat a hasty retreat up the street. A few shots were fired at our door and Lil, dragging out a .45 she had been given by a soldier, fired a few shots from the bathroom window after them. We were not bothered again.

The second night was a repeat of the first. We spent the day drinking and telling each other tales of our previous lives. Penny and I found mutual friends. My aunt and her aunt were neighbours. Yes, we were so desperate to ignore our present predicament we talked about our distant relatives. Boy, how desperate can you get?

Night fell suddenly, as it does in the tropics, and we lit candles to cook by. The mortars and rockets had been silent for a few hours and this seemed ominous. Who had won? What would become of us if the city had been taken? Was the Schwartz family alive and well? We lit our kerosene stove and dangerously barbecued steaks on forks, sitting in a circle around it.

'Just like a marshmallow roast back home,' said Kerry, and her eyes filled with tears.

So we had another drink.

About 9pm, we heard a vehicle roar up to our door and a loud banging on our French shutters.

'Open up, girls, open up, quick.' It was Kerry's dad, Phil, who had come to get us in a Vietnamese taxi, a tiny Renault. We blew out the candles and raced outside into the cool night air. Bundled in the taxi, we took off in a mad race across Cholon into Saigon to the Schwartz home. I tried to keep my head down, but the flickering of firelight on the glass window made me peek out. It seemed as if every second or third house was on fire. It was a miracle that our house had not been hit. I could see bodies in the street and this time they were not dogs. We were going so fast I caught only flashes of scenes lit by dancing fires. Here a burnt-out truck, there an ugly gaping hole where a house had been. Two or three bodies in a heap, looking inelegant in the way they were lying. The whole night smelt of gunfire and a smell I was later to know as that of death.

We travelled along Tran Hoang Quan, along Hung Vuong and across Hong Thap Tu around into Dinh Phung, the street where the Schwartz villa was situated. As we passed the Golden Hotel in Hong Thap Tu, there was a burst of gunfire and two men fell backwards out into the street. Phil, cursing aloud, held his foot flat to the floor and we whizzed around the corner out of immediate danger from stray bullets. We pulled into the driveway, and Mr Duc, the owner of the house ran from where he had been waiting in the shadows and unlocked the big iron gates to allow the car into the courtyard. Not a word was said as he locked the gates and we hustled out of the taxi into the house.

Mrs Schwartz burst into tears when she saw us and ran immediately to Kerry and clutched her daughter to her breast. We went upstairs, feeling our way in the darkened house. Pamela drew shutters and lit a candle and we sat down to hot coffee laced with brandy. Phil told us that he and Pamela and the entire Duc family had spent most of the past three days in the hallway, which they had lined with mattresses. After coffee, we put out the candle and all stepped out onto the balcony to look up and down the street. Phil told us that he had been standing there the previous night when he saw a rocket come over his roof and straight along the road about 9 metres above the surface. It hit the Dutch Embassy a few houses away on the opposite side of the street, blowing off the top front balcony and half a room. He didn't know if anyone had been hurt.

Once again, we bedded down in silence under mattresses.

On the fourth morning as we gathered for breakfast, Phil grew quite excited when he was able to tune in to an AFVN News broadcast on the radio. But the news was terrible. The City of Saigon, Cholon and outlying districts had been taken by North Vietnamese troops assisted by Vietcong. Fierce street fighting had occurred, the US bringing in tanks and troops to try to quell the rioting. Vietcong had tunnelled through the perimeters and up into the streets and it appeared that the entire underground of the racecourse in Cholon had been a secret VC arsenal. There were many dead and injured. Any listener who was injured was advised to wait for medical aid if possible. If urgent help was needed, the injured were to be taken to Third Field Hospital near the airport or to the 218th Medical Detachment or the Dental Clinic near the Golden Hotel. Apart from that, it appeared as if the city was once more in the hands of the established government, but we were all to stay indoors until an assessment could be made and cleaning up procedures established.

It was stressed that there was still danger in the streets, so we settled down once again for a day of confinement. Phil and Pamela told us as much as they knew of the history of Vietnam and we discussed the war, why we were here and if we were really doing the right thing by the Vietnamese people.

Phil's job was as an engineer with RMK-BRJ, and he was overseeing the building of highways, dams and other major engineering words. This work was being supplied to the people of Vietnam compliments of Uncle Sam, in an effort to stabilise the country so that the desire of some for communism would lessen. Phil said, as he understood it, that if the US could help maintain a stable government, increase prosperity and provide a reasonable standard of living for all the nationals, then the people who assisted the NVA and VC would gradually come to realise that life was OK and there would be no need for them to try to alter it. It all sounded so simple, and so right. But I felt that, although the theory was good, in practice, the Americans did not follow through. They did not treat the Vietnamese as equals, they stole from their own government (the military and the PX stores), they perpetuated the black market, they abused Vietnamese women and generally behaved like conquering heroes. No, I argued, it was not the Vietnamese who needed education to bring about a higher standard of living; it was the Americans who needed to be taught the truths of equality!

Towards evening, a further news broadcast was made, in which we were told that those with indoor jobs could attend to them on the morrow, provided they had private transport to work. Phil offered to drive us girls to work and, I must say, for once, I was eager to be back at the office and to catch up on everyone else's experiences. It was decided that we four girls would go to work the next day and proceed home from there if it was considered safe.

Pamela bustled about her kitchen and produced an excellent meal of lobster tails in butter sauce, pepper steaks and salad followed by good old Sara Lee pies. Phil opened a bottle of French champagne and we sat around the table feeling very thankful and very alive. We raised our glasses in a toast to Tet and to the Vietnamese people, and to our own survival through the worst Tet Offensive in the history of the war. We did not yet know about the massacre at Hue, nor about the deaths of many of our fellow workers and our friends, but that night we did know that we were all safe and well. It was a beautiful feeling.

Chapter Four

ALL PLAY AND NO WORK

I NEVER DID see Ricky B. Mansing III again. After his trip to Australia in mid-1967 to recruit Third Country National staff to work for the Post Exchange system, the Filipino contingent of the workforce buzzed with dissatisfaction and they took the opportunity of the Tet Offensive to put out a 'contract' on him: $US1,000 to get rid of him, in any way. He was lucky. He heard about the contract just two days before Tet and made hurried and secretive arrangements to leave the country permanently.

Let me explain the pecking order of the US Department of Defence direct-hire program: the Vietnamese people, called Local Nationals (LNs), were ranked number one, because, after all, it was *their* country. Ranked Number Two was any US citizen. Number Three, or Third Country Nationals (TCNs), were Filipinos, Thais, Koreans and Chinese nationals hired in-country to assist in the operation of the vast PX conglomerate. The PX system was the third-largest retail organisation in the world behind Woolworths and Sears Roebuck.

In previous times, the PX had operated from America, taking to war only those items considered vital to the welfare of the fighting man. But this war was different. It was the first time the PX had moved lock, stock and barrel into a war zone and set up shop. Not many American civilians were interested in working in Vietnam and, consequently, staffing the administrative side of the PX with English-speaking underlings was difficult. The engineers and mechanics, for example, who did come from America to work found it almost impossible to impart instructions to the Asian TCNs, partly because of language difficulties, and partly because the Filipinos, Koreans and Thais did not have the expertise needed to do their jobs. Consequently, Ricky Mansing was sent to Australia to recruit Aussies — as engineers, mechanics, airconditioning experts, managers for the snack bars, food retailers, retail managers, electronics experts, administrative assistants, secretaries — and me. I did not seem to fit in anywhere. I hated what the Americans termed 'secretarial' work. As far as I was concerned, I was a typist who was expected to turn out the grand sum of at least three pages a day. The Americans had no idea of what a secretary was, in my books. Now, as any Australian secretary will confirm and, in fact, as any foreign employer will confirm, we are the best secretaries in the world ... and I was being wasted. I felt very frustrated. So I spent most of my days chatting to soldiers, wandering around the offices and sometimes even waltzing out into town for a few hours to see the sights of Saigon. As time passed, my jaunts out of the office became longer and I was constantly amazed that no one said anything to me about them.

One day when I was up in the gods of the office building talking to Penny while she worked in Retail Branch, checking off an inventory, she stumbled over a word out loud:

'Tic 21,' she said, 'Pro … pro … pro …?'

I glanced over her shoulder.

'Prophylactics,' I said loudly, helpfully.

'Boy, what a mouthful!' she exclaimed.

The soldier sitting nearby started to snigger, then got up and wandered off to tell his mates about our lack of knowledge.

'What are they?' Penny asked.

'I think they're frogs, you know, Frenchies,' I answered.

'But they are supplied FREE to Australian soldiers,' she laughed.

'Fancy the Yanks selling them in the PX.'

We giggled some more, as neither of us had ever seen a soldier using one. We looked up the sales figures on Tic 21, 'Necessity Item — Prophylactics', and sure enough, there were record sales.

'Now we know what's really going on out in the field,' we chortled. We decided to keep a close watch on the sales figures for this particular item from now on.

We decided to wander down to the snack bar for coffee and, when we entered, the word had spread of our ignorance as to the meaning of the word prophylactic, and some of the guys cat-called, 'Hey, Penny, wanna see how they work?' Someone threw a packet at her, which she caught deftly.

'I will keep this as a reminder of my tour of Vietnam,' she announced. 'It is fitting, after all. An *unopened* packet of Tic 21s really says it all!'

On one of my jaunts around the office I came across the Public Information Office (PIO). It fascinated me.

It was a happy band of mixed races, all busy the entire day, producing two newspapers. One, the *Vietnam Regional Exchange Voice*, was a fortnightly employee newspaper, and the other was issued on alternate fortnights and was called *Exchange News*. The latter was the organ through which the PX advised all troops in-country of goods available, services supplied and other interesting facets of life in Vietnam. The information office comprised an Officer in Charge or OIC (a designated military captain or lieutenant); an editor, who was an American civilian; one Third Country National reporter (this position was held by Lito Ermita, a Filipino); one US military reporter (this was Spec. Five Ben Hanson); a TCN photographer (Bernard Roblis, a Filipino); a TCN secretary (Marie Sameos, a Filipina); and a troubleshooter officially called a photographer, Sergeant Rhee, a mean-looking Korean-born American who was more like a Mafioso than a sergeant. I felt that the office badly needed an Australian.

I tentatively brought the subject up with Captain Morris, the OIC, who agreed with me wholeheartedly. But there was not enough work for two secretaries.

'Oh,' I said nonchalantly, 'I'm really a journalist.' I crossed my fingers behind my back.

'Oh,' he was interested. 'Who did you work for in Sydney?'

'The Australian *Women's Weekly*.' I said the first thing that came into my head. 'Circulation one and a half million.'

'Terrific. I'll fix it then,' Capt. Morris said, and he did.

Within the week, he had impressed on Colonel Verona that he really needed another reporter in the PIO, he had the Manning Document altered, and I was given a new job — one that took me all over the country on story searches. I could not have been happier. I couldn't write … but I couldn't have been happier!

Reporter Ben Hanson and I became firm friends. He smoked pot all day long (in the office) and wrote poetry. He told me he had spent the four days of Tet in an opium den, which he described as just fantastic, except now he couldn't concentrate on his writing. He took me back to the funny little attic room he rented in a seedy district of Cholon, and introduced me to Bob, an 'Indian'. Bob was a deserter from the army, and he looked like a skeleton after so much drug-taking. He spent all day lying on a pallet in a daze, and I didn't particularly like him because he couldn't communicate very well. I suppose it was the effect of the drugs. Hanson lit a burner and put some plasticine stuff in a spoon, which he held over the flame till it melted. He gave the spoon to Bob who took it over into a corner and huddled over it — I suppose fixing a needle or something for himself. Hanson then pinched off a bit more of this 'hash' and swallowed it whole. I waited. Nothing seemed to happen to

him. After a while he became very animated and put a Jose
Feliciano record (*Come On Baby, Light My Fire*) on the
record player.

He started crooning to me, 'Come on, baby', and took
me by the hand, pulling me to my feet. We danced a slow,
rhythmic dance and he placed his cigarette between my lips.
I dragged deeply, holding the smoke as long as I could, as
I had seen him do. It tasted sweet and strong. I exhaled,
expecting lights to burst in my head or something, but
nothing happened. It was a non-event. We sat down on the
mats on the floor and listened to some more records —
Feliciano, Ike and Tina Turner, The Animals. I had two
reefers during this time and several cans of Coke to wash
away the funny taste. Still nothing happened to me. I decided
that pot was not all it was cracked up to be ... I felt no
different, just, well, smooth (like my movements were
gliding) and a little sleepy. I suppose you could say I had
a sense of wellbeing.

On the short walk back to the office, I found that
I was ravenous. I checked in to the PIO, then made my way
immediately upstairs to the snack bar to get a sandwich.
I bought a toasted cheese and ham in a paper bag and took it
back downstairs to the office to eat while I was working. I sat
in front of my typewriter, gazing at the blank paper and
concentrating on what I was going to write, all the while
eating my sandwich from my lap.

When I finished eating, I looked for the paper bag to
throw it in the bin, but I couldn't find it. Realisation

dawned! I had eaten the bloody thing. I was so high I had
forgotten to take the sandwich out of the bag and had sat
there stupidly munching away, devouring (and thoroughly
enjoying) paper and all. Hanson nearly wet himself with joy
when I told him. He wrote a poem about it.

Our translator in the PIO, who translated the *VRE
Voice* into Vietnamese for the LN staff, was Miss Nguyen, an
elegant gracious Vietnamese girl of 21. Nguyen, Marie (the
Filipina secretary) and I became firm friends. We had set our
office up to be completely self-contained. Capt. Morris
arranged (with able assistance from Sgt Rhee) to have
builders come in and knock down walls to make a darkroom,
a photo lab, editor's office, main office (where we underlings
sat) and, joy of joys, our very own toilet. The toilets in the
other parts of the building were a sight to behold. Because of
the lack of refrigeration in the country, the Vietnamese
purchased all their foodstuffs on the hoof if possible. So to go
to the toilet, one had to step carefully over a gaggle of ducks
tethered to the basin pipes, two or three pans of water
containing lobsters and fat carp and maybe a cage or two of
pigs. The toilets themselves were fun. When one pulled the
chain, the water rose swiftly in the bowl to within an inch
of the top rim, swirled vivaciously, then whooshed away with
a sucking sound. On every second or third flush, however,
the bowl overflowed. The Vietnamese never put paper in the
bowl; they put soiled toilet paper in a bin next to the toilet.
Apart from the foul smell of the room, it was most
unpleasant to tiptoe through the overflow on the floor —

wet, messy and poopy with bits of used paper floating in it. Yuk.

We tried to keep our Public Information Office Toilet (called the 'PIO Poo House') secret, but word soon spread, and Kerry, Penny and Lil used it, as well as Chantou and some Vietnamese secretaries. They were all solemnly sworn in, with raised hand, to put paper in the bowl, to press the button once only, and not to keep animals in the room.

In vain, we Aussies and Kerry tried to talk Marie and Nguyen into coming to a party at Phu Loi with us. Nguyen's refusal I could understand. She could hardly socialise and enjoy herself while her country was at war and, as she was from a good family, she would bring disgrace to her father if she mixed freely with soldiers. But Marie was one of us, a TCN, and we didn't give up hope that she would accompany us on a chopper trip one weekend. She had a good friend to whom she introduced us, named Carmen Arcega, also a Filipina. Over the years in Vietnam, Carmen became the most well-known female in the country. If you wanted anything, Carmen could get it for you, or knew someone who could help. She had personality plus, a real life force and drive. We loved her. She joined our happy band of weekend travellers and, from then on, the world was ours. Carmen organised chopper rides to other parts of the country; she organised parties for us from Da Nang to Con Son Island in the south. She introduced me to a colonel in Saigon who took me to Bangkok for the weekend on a U-21, a small Lear jet (military, of course). We stayed at the Siam

Intercontinental Hotel and I got food poisoning from the curry and spoiled the weekend. I promised the colonel a raincheck.

On one of our weekend jaunts, we girls went to the 25th Infantry Division base at Cu Chi, to the west of Saigon in an area called the Parrot's Beak. It was quite close to the Cambodian border and was considered to be a really dangerous area, as the Division Headquarters were situated on the old Michelin rubber plantation, smack in the middle of the Ho Chi Minh trail. The commander had organised food and drink in the upstairs part of the old plantation house. We arrived by helicopter and were smuggled under cover of dusk into waiting jeeps and driven to the house. Penny, Kerry, Carmen and I were shown our room and we showered (cold water) and changed. We had pretty long dresses for the occasion. When we went into the party room, as usual, we were the only girls present. The room opened onto a balcony and we sat outside in the night air, enjoying the cool and talking to the guys. Most of them hadn't seen a white female for months and we were all plied with questions. Music started up and we danced, changing partners every few minutes so that we could try at least to dance with them all.

I loved these parties every Saturday night. It was absolutely wonderful being able to say, like the queer at church when given the choice of hymns, 'I'll have him, and him and him.' Every American soldier was good-looking — no kidding. They were all tanned, virile, masculine, tall, gorgeous and horny. Oh, the choice we had! But as usual, we had to be careful. I finally made a choice that night of Joe, who had only six weeks left in-country. We left the party discreetly (or as discreetly as possible with 50 pairs of eyes watching us) and made our way to Joe's hootch. He was lovely — unhurried, and a good lover. We made love time and time again, talking, laughing and snuggling in his narrow army cot. I promised to come to Cu Chi again the next Saturday night.

I really liked Joe; we suited each other. I could see at least my next five Saturday nights would be spent with him, if I could possibly arrange it, but, as we girls had been smuggled into camp, we had to be careful not to be seen by too many people. Next morning, Joe and some other fellows took us on a swift ride around the division in a covered jeep and then we went back to our 'official' room to shower and change for the trip home. We had breakfast and then a soldier came in to say the chopper was ready for us. We kissed our fellows goodbye (Carmen always managed to bed the commanding officer wherever we went) and off we headed home. On the trip back, the chopper pilot dropped low and gave us a commentary on the progress of the war. We all wore helmets with microphones and earphones in them so we could communicate easily above the noise of the blades.

Back in Saigon, we landed on the Free World Forces helipad close to home — a much nicer landing place than way out the back of Tan San Nhut Airport. We were only a cyclo ride away from our house. As we raced from the helipad, waving goodbye to our pilot and gunners in the chopper, we were observed quietly by an American colonel, who took a notepad from his pocket and jotted down the number of the chopper.

On Monday in the office, a phone call came through for me from Joe in Cu Chi. Over the static in the line, I heard him say that they were in trouble for having civilians in the chopper. I said I would try to find out what had happened and smooth things over for them. I hung up and immediately went to see Carmen — Miss Fix-It. She rang Free World Forces Headquarters and, from a friend of hers there, discovered the name of the colonel who was kicking up the fuss. His name was Colonel Revis. That afternoon, Carmen set off determinedly down to FWF HQ in her prettiest dress. She came back grinning from ear to ear and announced that there would be no more trouble from Colonel Revis — in fact, from now on, we could use the helipad whenever we wanted. A cheer went up from the girls. I don't know how she did it, but Carmen had come through. God, I admired her.

I rang Joe. This sounds simple, but it took more than two hours to get through and the line was dreadful. It faded in and out and the static was worse than usual. He wanted to know the name of the colonel.

'Revis,' I shouted.

'What?'

'Revis.'

'What?'

'Revis,' I was going blue in the face.

'Spell phonetically please?'

I was stuck.

Hanson, who had been listening, grabbed the phone from my hand.

'RAPE EVERY VIRGIN IN SAIGON,' he shouted, and handed the phone back to me.

'Christ,' said Joe, 'I certainly got THAT.'

The next Saturday night, Carmen, Penny and I made the trip to Cu Chi. Carmen smiled mysteriously and announced that she had organised for the chopper to collect us from the Free World Forces helipad. There was no further fuss made about us using this very convenient inner-city landing spot.

When we arrived, Joe and Penny's man, Bill, ran out to meet us carrying ponchos. 'Quick, hide under these,' they said. Word had spread of our visit the previous weekend and the camp commander was furious, so we had to be really careful and be kept under wraps from then on. This visit was really undercover. Carmen, in grand style, stalked into the waiting jeep and arranged herself in the front seat. We drove off across the bumpy roads to our company's area and disbursed quickly to our hootches — Carmen to the colonel's and Penny and I to one cunningly organised to be shared by Joe and Bill. We were there for the night — no party this week. We four had our own party. The boys had stolen canned hams, bologna sausage and plenty of booze, and we feasted, played cards and went to bed early. Once again, Joe was simply beautiful. We were right in the middle of being beautiful with each other when the rockets started coming in. We sat up. Penny and Bill in the other bed sat up and we switched on a flashlight.

'Sounds close,' said Bill.

'Better get to the bunker,' said Joe.

'No way,' said Penny and I.

We dressed 'just in case', and sat nervously smoking in the half-light. Then the siren went. Red Alert. The perimeter had been breached. We had to go to the bunker, with all the other guys. We would be discovered!

Penny and I were still hesitating when a rocket landed really close to us, moving us into shaky action. We followed the boys as fast as we could across the dark compound towards a bunker. I could see the sandbagged roof gleaming dully in the starlight. I was puffing from nervous exhaustion; my legs wouldn't go fast enough. Penny was a long-legged lady and she raced ahead frantically. She reached the top of the bunker steps, paused dramatically, then fell headfirst down the stairs into the bunker. You should have seen the faces on the soldiers sitting huddled in the bunker. They didn't know what had struck them. They had no idea there were girls on the base, let alone an Aussie blonde in a miniskirt who fell, with her dress around her ears, into their midst. 'Christ,' one muttered, 'I must be dreaming.'

After the raid was over, Penny and I (Carmen had not appeared) were taken to the division commander's tent and were asked how we had got there. 'I'm a reporter,' I said, showing my ID card, 'and I'm doing a story search for my magazine.'

'Who brought you here?' the Commander thundered.

'No one,' we said.

He kept at us, shouting angry questions. We denied ever having been there before and stuck to our story of being women's magazine reporters doing a story. Finally, he said we could leave in the morning and told the adjutant to find quarters for us. The adjutant looked like a nice guy and we conned him into letting us go back to the company, where we told Joe and Bill everything was OK. But we slept in a chaste state for the rest of the night in the VIP quarters. Next morning, the division commander laid on a chopper for us and, with brilliant timing, Carmen was smuggled aboard too. It was our last trip to Cu Chi for many months.

The next Saturday night we stayed in Saigon. The word spread quickly and, by 6pm, when we were about to leave the office, a couple of jeeps were outside with some air force guys we had never met sitting in them.

One, a young captain, introduced himself and offered to drive us home while we got changed for a party they were putting on in our honour at the Tan San Nhut air base. We agreed immediately, fitted ourselves in between the boys and were driven home. We showered and changed while the boys had a drink. I was joined in the shower by a rather lovely fellow named Chuck and we lathered each other up and joked about what would happen if we dropped the soap. So we did!

The party at the air base was really in honour of General Dickson, the top dog of the 7th Air Force, Pacific.

I had heard that the general was a shit and that none of the boys liked him. He strutted around the party room looking the girls over. Penny had found herself a lovely little first lieutenant and was dancing close to him, almost making love on the dance floor. General Dickson spotted them and marched over to break in, tapping the young lieutenant on the shoulder. He stepped back with deference, but Penny grabbed him and pulled him back into her arms.

'Piss off, General,' she said loudly.

The ensuing silence was thick.

As usual, the party was spoiled halfway through by incoming rockets and mortars and we all made our way outside to take cover in the bunkers. One air force captain, a pilot, was so pissed he shouted something about getting out and fighting the bastards, and ran outside and climbed into his plane. He tried to take off and, in front of our horrified eyes, the plane slewed sideways and crashed, bursting into flames on the runway. Some men started to run towards the plane, but they were beaten back by the flames. No one could have survived that inferno. The sirens were still giving out Red Alert. I was undecided whether to follow the main crowd into the bunkers or to stay and watch what happened with the crashed plane, when I saw a group of pilots talking animatedly together and pointing to the plane. A couple broke away and ran to get fire hydrants. They raced up the runway and sprayed the plane down. More joined them. I saw them pull the pilot's body clear, then, with a repeating rifle, fire shots into the plane and the body which jerked with each impact. I was horrified and raced to the bunker, shouting about what I had seen to all and sundry.

An officer grabbed me by the shoulders and shook me, saying to me firmly, 'Take it easy, there's a good reason for that.' He quietly explained to me that war insurance did not cover self-inflicted death. The dead pilot had a wife and two children in the States. The fellows had done the shooting to make it look as though the pilot had died as a result of enemy action and I was not to tell a soul about what I had seen or else the widow would not collect the insurance, and the memory of her husband would be tainted also.

I sat in the bunker wondering about the friendship of those pilots for their dead comrade and feeling grief for the widow and her children. When the All Clear sounded, I came out to find that Penny had organised General Joseph's driver to take us home in his big black bulletproof car. The General was spending his usual weekend in Bangkok with his wife.

The drive home was not pleasant, as Saigon had been attacked again by Vietcong. The next day would be my first free Sunday in Saigon and I had planned to see what went on in the city on the Vietnamese workers' day off. I hoped that the war wasn't going to interfere with my sightseeing. Even though we all accepted having to avoid danger at every turn, it would be nice to walk the streets and pretend it was a normal city.

Chapter Five

ON ANY SUNDAY?

I HAD BEEN in the country for four and a half months and had not yet seen fully the beautiful city of Saigon. I had had various trips to restaurants, including the world-class Mayfair Restaurant (best French onion soup in the world) and to bars around town, but usually in the dark and with a crowd of friends. I had seen the usual tourist sights, too, on my jaunts out from the office during working hours. But I had not yet spent daylight leisure time in the city and I was looking forward to our planned trip to the zoo, followed by lunch and perhaps a cyclo ride out of town a little way to see a famous Buddhist pagoda.

Unfortunately, none of us knew that that day, 19 May, was Ho Chi Minh's birthday. The Vietcong and anti-government factions had planned their own Sunday in Saigon.

We set off in pedicabs, Kerry and I in one, Penelope and Lil in another. We had our *papasans* drop us in Tu Do

(Freedom) Street, right in the heart of Saigon. In the central square was a park and fountain and, opposite the Continental Palace Hotel (where Graham Greene wrote *The Quiet American*), were many vendors' stalls selling black market electronic equipment and US military-issue clothing and changing money at good rates. The going rate was $US1 for 118 piastres, but we got 240 piastres for each $US1 Military Payment Certificate because we charmed the vendor and said in Vietnamese, 'We are Australians, Cheap Charlies.' Thus, with plenty of local money in hand, we examined the displays of oil paintings and lacquer-work vases and artefacts. I bought a painting and a black vase embossed with golden flowers.

We wandered south-west and it was getting close to lunchtime when the smell of roast pork reached our noses. My mouth started to water. We decided that we would eat from a street vendor's stand (in spite of official frowns on such activity) and walked towards the delicious smell. A small crowd was gathered at the corner and we expected this to be where the vendor was. It certainly was where the beautiful pork smell was coming from.

As we approached, the crowd parted to reveal what appeared to be, at first glance, a smoking black stump. A couple of saffron-robed priests were standing either side of it, chanting. I stared, comprehending slowly. Kerry, beside me, gasped and turned away, vomiting. I felt my stomach start to heave. I could see legs in a lotus position, the skin blackened and splitting wide, revealing an entire thighbone.

The black hands, crossed in the lap, had stark white bones sticking out from the ends of the fingers. As I watched, the skin, still smouldering, shrivelled and peeled from the shoulders.

We turned and ran from the awful scene. The silent crowd closed behind us.

I was crying and shaking and had to sit in the gutter. Penny, Lil and Kerry were in the same state, and we sat there for ages, shocked. Finally, Penny, always the one to pull herself up, said, 'Come on, let's get out,' and we hurried back the way we had come. We heard later that it was a 24-year-old Buddhist nun who had self-immolated in protest against the Thieu regime and Catholic persecution of Buddhists.

I desperately wanted to see and hear English-speaking people, my own kind, and we walked quickly back to the centre of Saigon, still silent, still shocked.

At the International House, a few doors down from the United Servicemen's Organisation canteen on Nguyen Hue Street, we stopped. Kerry, being an American, was a member of the I-House and said she would sign us in as there was a good bar upstairs, but we met the usual official prejudice. Kerry was allowed to sign only one person in. I queried the policy angrily.

'Only American military and civilians allowed,' the doorman said.

'But I work for the US Department of Defence,' I almost shouted, frustrated and again near tears. 'All we want is a drink in your bloody bar.'

'Now lady,' the doorman said, 'if you were a foreign journalist I could let you in.'

'Done,' I shouted, and slapped my ID card down in front of him. That job in the Public Information Office was certainly opening doors for me.

I signed in the spare 'undesirable' and we made our way upstairs to the bar. It was a dark room and the airconditioning was icy after the stifling heat of the streets outside. When my eyes got used to the dark, I noticed a horseshoe-shaped bar and many tables and chairs about the room. Subtle lighting from concealed pelmets lent a seductive air, the carpet was thick, the chairs wool upholstered and the entire place was crowded with gorgeous men. As usual, we were the only girls present.

The horseshoe-shaped bar turned out to be a piano bar, so we pulled up stools and ordered drinks. As the drinks arrived, a fellow at a table close by signalled the waiter he would pay, so we raised our glasses to him in thanks.

Oh, lovely, lovely booze. A bourbon and Coke took the shakes away (were we all becoming alcoholics?). A Filipino holding a guitar seated himself behind the piano and started to play and sing. He was fantastically good. At any time, I'm a sucker for my own private entertainer and, taking the opportunity of a break in his songs, I went round the bar and sat next to him, plying him with requests. *La Malagana, El Rancho Grande, Besame Mucho.* He obliged and I shut my eyes; I was in another world. He then swung into *Waltzing Matilda* and was greeted by loud applause from our small contingent. He introduced himself as Mario and said he was an ex-member of the Trios Los Panchos, a famous group. I was thrilled. He really chased away my worries that afternoon.

Three fellows had joined the other girls, so I bought Mario a drink and moved back to my friends. The fellows were Green Berets and introduced themselves as Jim Ward (Major), Bill Hull and Alan Roberts. Jim was telling the girls about the Tet Offensive. He had been at Khe San, right in the middle of fierce fighting. We went on to talk about the politics of the country, the graft and the black market. All three spoke Vietnamese fluently, so for once I listened with respect. These were guys who certainly knew what it was all about.

'The Tet ceasefire was due to start on 29 January,' said Jim, 'but, as you all know, it was cancelled due to the offensive, which started on 30 January. Saigon and Hue, the ancient Imperial City and a major objective as far as the North Vietnamese were concerned, were attacked simultaneously on 31 January. We were fighting in the provinces until 24 February and street fighting still erupted in Saigon right up until 23 February,' he told us. We hadn't noticed! Life had continued as normal for us girls. We had realised that there was danger in the streets right up to 5 February, but after that we were not collected and taken to work by private vehicle anymore. Christ, I thought, another official fuck-up. We had moved freely around Saigon and Cholon for two and a half weeks after that and no one had bothered to tell us to be careful.

Bill had been stationed just outside Saigon before the offensive and had been rushed in as part of the airborne troops who relieved the city. 'The attack on Saigon actually began on 31 January at 3am,' he told us. 'Within hours, the Presidential Palace had been blown up and Radio Saigon was held for 24 hours by enemy troops. They attacked the Navy Headquarters, the Philippine Embassy and three bachelor officers' quarters. About 5,000 Cong, it is estimated, travelled into Saigon just prior to Tet on the pretext of family reunions for the holiday. They were armed from arsenals within the city.'

'An army friend of mine was killed at the US Embassy,' I said. 'What actually happened there? I get conflicting reports whenever I ask anyone.'

Alan answered me. 'Twenty Vietcong were detailed especially to take the US Embassy. They blew a hole in the wall and moved across the grounds. A chopper tried to land on the roof to offload wounded American military, but the Cong drove it off with gunfire. Then the US Airborne troops landed another chopper on the roof and came out fighting! They killed 19 Vietcong and captured the one survivor. My marine friend was on guard duty that day and was shot by the Cong, along with a civilian Vietnamese lady.'

'Christ,' muttered Penny, 'five *thousand* infiltrators. That's about 17 battalions!'

'Yes,' Jim continued. 'They hid out in the An Quang Pagoda and issued arms from there. Also more than 4,000 local resident civilians assisted the Cong.'

'That's why *Mamasan* and Van stayed out all night,' Kerry whispered to me.

'And that's probably why we were not harmed in the house-to-house fighting,' I whispered back. '*Mamasan* and Van like us and I bet that's what the White Mouse was checking on too.'

Jim was astounded that we hadn't read the local papers … until he checked himself, realising that we didn't read Vietnamese. None of the Americans we knew read Vietnamese either, so it was no wonder we hadn't known fully what happened. The official version given out through MACV leaflets played the whole thing down.

'Then you don't know what happened at Hue?' Jim asked. We shook our heads.

'On 1 February, the US infantry and tanks entered Saigon, and government troops recaptured Radio Saigon. There were tanks, armoured cars and mortars in the street-fighting, which continued until the VC withdrew to the Gia Dinh area, where the Green Berets' headquarters are situated. By 7 February, the fighting was practically contained to the Phu Tho racecourse, and the B52s bombed the closest to the city they had ever done, within 10 miles of Saigon. A small new offensive started up on 18 February, when Cong attempted to take Tan San Nhut air base and White Mouse headquarters. The air base was rocketed badly on the night of 19 February.'

'I can imagine,' said Lil. 'We were at a party there last night and the same thing happened again.' We proceeded to tell of the drunk pilot crashing on the runway.

'Get to Hue,' Kerry was impatient.

'Ok,' Jim sighed. He ordered more drinks. We were a captive audience, unaware of time.

When the drinks arrived, he leaned back in his chair and asked, 'How are your stomachs?'

'Dreadful,' we chorused, and told him of the Buddhist self-immolation we had just witnessed.

'Well, something just as horrible happened at Hue during Tet and the enormity of the horror is just now becoming known,' he said. 'It wasn't until the end of April that official figures became available and only after soldiers had stumbled over depressions in the ground and we had started digging did we know what had happened up there.

'Over a dozen mass graves have been discovered just outside the Perfumed City, which is the ancient part of Hue. This Imperial City is of great significance to the Vietnamese. The Viets have always controlled this part of the world, but in 111 BC their kingdom of Nam Viet was conquered by the Chinese. The Trung sisters, leading a revolt on an elephant's back, drove out the Chinese in 43 AD and triumphantly entered the city of Hue. In a few years though, the Chinese returned, and the Trung sisters committed suicide by throwing themselves into the Perfumed River. Hue is considered the national birthplace of Vietnam, and is really a type of holy city. As far as I can see it, the Viets are still trying to throw out the Chinese and I am here to assist them.

'But back to the massacre. When the graves were uncovered, there were the bodies of more than 1,000 civilians there, some of them tied together. They had been shot, beheaded and some of them were buried alive by the Vietcong and North Vietnamese Army troops. The victims included political leaders, civil servants, teachers, workers, merchants, policeman, students, schoolchildren, women and some foreigners, including three German doctors, two French priests, three Koreans and one British subject from Hong Kong.'

'God,' I breathed, 'no wonder that White Mouse Chief, General Nhuyen Ngoc Loan, shot that VC in the head in the street just after Tet. Bastards. They are supposed to be on the side of the ordinary Viet. This must have really hurt the Vietcong cause, this Hue business, I mean.'

'Not really,' said Jim. 'Their propaganda denies the blame for the Hue massacre. They are telling the Viets that the Americans did it.' He shrugged. 'Until the American learns to speak Vietnamese, to communicate with these people as equals, we haven't a chance of beating the Vietcong. They work with us during the day, we let them steal from us, we ourselves propagate the black market, which is all money going to their cause, and at night they laugh at us as fools and blow us up. The whole damn American official attitude stinks.' He became moody.

Mario was beating out a fast rhumba, so I grabbed Jim's hand and led him to the small dance floor. 'Here,' he said, 'my gun is too heavy to dance with. Put it in your handbag please.' He removed the bullets, stuffing them into his pocket, and placed the gun in the bag I held open. It was bloody heavy. I made a mental note to remind him to reload when we left the I-House.

We were all hungry, so we moved into the large back room, which had a much bigger dance floor, a band and tiers of tables at which to dine. In one corner of the room, a salad bar was set up. I could not get used to the way Americans ate their salad first (with jello on the plate), then drank a glass of water and then ordered dinner. That night, I ordered prime rib of beef, which I had never had before, and wished afterwards that I hadn't been such a guts on the salad first. The size of the steak was out of this world, so Jim ordered a doggie bag for me and, after consuming many bottles of wine and dancing until curfew was sounded, I grabbed my doggie bag in one hand, Jim in the other and headed down the stairs.

Outside we climbed aboard the boys' jeep, which they had padlocked to a street post. They checked it thoroughly first for booby traps. Then we drove home to Cholon in the dark, quiet streets. Jim wanted to spend the night with me, but I put him off. I was drunk (and I like to be sober to enjoy it) and still a little shocked by the morning's events. So I gave him my work number and he said he would call me the next day.

I went to sleep, counting men: Joe, Jim, Virgil, rainchecked colonels in Bangkok, blackened hands in the lotus position with white bones poking out the ends.

The perimeter fire bases kept up their steady boom, boom, boom, lighting up the surrounds of my French doors with each 'boom'. It was only when I was nearly asleep that I remembered I had forgotten to give Jim back his .45 pistol. 'Hope he doesn't need it,' I thought dreamily, and passed out.

Chapter Six

THE DIAL-A-CHOPPER SERVICE

IN MY JOB as a reporter for the *Vietnam Regional Exchange Voice* and the *Exchange News*, I travelled at least once a week out of Saigon into the field on story searches. 'Into the field' sounds as though I was going into fighting areas; in fact, the outlying villages and military posts that I visited were relatively safe. During the day, life went on in the villages and little was seen of the war, but most nights Vietcong made raids or rocket attacks on the military posts. Constantly, there was the sound of the perimeter Howitzers, apparently firing aimlessly in the hope of hitting something or at least of keeping the Cong at bay throughout the night.

I had travelled on Travel Duty orders (TDY) to Dalat in the Central Highlands, where in outer areas there still existed the original Viets, or Montagnards (Mountain People) as the French had called them. They had wonderful cottage industries — weaving brightly coloured threads into jackets, shawls and waistcoats, beautiful wooden carvings, ivory carvings and the like. They lived in huts on high stilts for coolness and for protection from wild animals. Until then, I hadn't realised that the jungles of Vietnam contained such a profusion of wildlife. Tigers and elephants roamed freely, panda and a great variety of monkeys lived in the thick triple-canopied jungle highlands. Once I was staying on a Korean base and a Red Alert was sounded when mines on the perimeter defences were set off. The perimeter had been breached not by Cong, but by a very large and beautiful tiger. He was mutilated, but the Koreans chopped off his undamaged head and spent the entire morning taking turns at having their photo taken with one foot on the head. Korean bases were rarely troubled by Vietcong attacks. The Cong were terrified, and rightly so, of the very famous Black Panther Division of the Republic of Korea Army. Their White Horse Regiment was also feared. While staying with the Black Panther Division, the officer in charge of a company took me in his jeep on a regular sweep of the Vietnamese villages in his area. The villages were supposed to be hotbeds of Cong activity and I felt sorry for the poor village chieftain who had to contend with the Koreans in the day telling him to hand over the Vietcong members of his community and the Cong at night extracting boys and taxes for their cause. The poor man lived constantly under threat from both sides. I was told the expected reign of a village chieftain, in those times, was three months.

The company officer said that he had sent a contingent out to three villages the previous day and told the chiefs to have 20 Vietcong rounded up and ready to hand over, or there would be reprisals. His men had gone back that morning and there were no captured Cong ready to hand over to the Koreans and reprisals had been carried out against the village. We were to tour the three villages to inspect the effect of the reprisals.

As we entered the village, I recognised the smell of death. I started to wish I hadn't come on the trip. As we entered the village square, Korean soldiers came forward pushing a very distressed old man who I assumed was the village chief. Through an interpreter, the officer and the chief talked, with much nodding on the part of the chief. Then we walked through the houses to the rear of the compound and there, sticking out of the ground, were four bamboo poles about 2.5 metres high, on top of which were four Viet heads. Blood had run down the poles and was dark on the ground and flies buzzed around. The heads were crawling with flies. Little children peeped around the houses and an agitated woman came and shoed them away.

I turned on my heel and quickly walked back to the jeep. When the officer rejoined me, I told him I didn't wish to continue the inspection tour, that I had seen enough, thank you. He looked at me, grinning. 'White girl not so strong, eh?' he said, and ordered one of the convoy jeeps to take me back to base camp.

I had to travel on one trip from Saigon to Dalat and to Ban Me Thout in the west, and the only flight I could get on was a KIA (Killed In Action) flight. I waited at Dalat

Airport beside rows of coffins and dark green plastic-looking sacks. The coffins contained the bodies of dead Vietnamese, and the sacks American bodies. They were laid out on pallets in orderly rows. When the plane landed, the bodies were loaded, all with the heads facing the cockpit, all face up, and none overlapping. The plane stank of death — a sickly sweet, vomity smell. It clung to my clothing after I had landed in Ban Me Thout.

Some of my TDY trips were tedious and lonely. I always had plenty of fellows to talk to and who were happy to share their table with me. Most of them offered to share their bed as well, but I rarely took them up on it. If I had to stay overnight out of Saigon on TDY, I usually put up in a local hotel or, in the absence of civilian amenities, the VIP quarters of the nearest base camp. I lined up with the guys and ate in the mess halls. No one ever queried my 'right' to eat US Army food, at least not at that stage. The food was nearly always good and wholesome. Breakfast was a choice of bacon, eggs done any way (powdered eggs always had to be scrambled, but in some places the eggs were fresh, supplied from local farms), ham, pancakes, maple syrup, hominy grits. I ate like the Americans, piling everything onto one plate. Eggs and maple syrup are nice!

During the first week of June 1968, I was told to do a story about the boys on Nui Ba Den, the Black Virgin Mountain. It was a mountain shaped like a pyramid, sticking straight up out of the rubber plantation at Dau Tieng, west of Saigon. And joy of joys, the nearest base camp where I would stay overnight was the 25th Infantry Division, since moved from Cu Chi. The mountain afforded such a good lookout that a company was stationed permanently on its tip, reporting by radio back to the 25th Division of any suspect movements in the plantation below. I suppose the mountain was about 8km from the base camp and I was to be flown in by chopper from Dau Tieng. Hanson was to accompany me, as he was a soldier and could carry a gun and could protect me if need be. The Vietcong had started another major offensive in early June and it was a pretty dangerous time to be trotting off to Nui Ba Den.

The stupid thing was that Hanson refused point-blank to carry a rifle or pistol — he would rather smoke pot and write poetry. I patted him on the arm and told him not to worry, I still had Jim Ward's .45 pistol. So Hanson got an issue of ammunition (the issuing officer couldn't understand why he didn't want to sign out a pistol as well) and we typed up our travel orders. Kerry, in Administrative Branch, was the one who organised the photocopying of the orders. When I got mine back, I typed up another set and, with shaky hand, forged the commander's signature on them. This set was in the name of Penelope Jones and the 'reason for travel' was typed in neatly — 'story search' — the same as on my and Manson's orders. Kerry waited till a quiet time, then ran off the copies, sneaking them back to me during a coffee break. I raced upstairs, grabbed Penny and dragged her to the ladies' room. 'Start looking sick,' I told her. 'We're off to Dau Tieng for a couple of days.'

Penny did a good job, visiting the ladies' room at least five more times that afternoon. Finally, she went to the Retail Manager's office and told him she had Ho Chi Minh's Revenge and should be sent home. He was most concerned and had her driven home in the commander's car. Hanson came home from work with me, we packed bags quickly and, with great excitement, set off to the airport. Hanson didn't take a change of clothes. He took a plastic bag full of pot, three cameras, an ammunition belt with four clips in it, no money, his travel orders and his sunglasses. I had to carry his pen and clipboard.

It seemed strange getting a regular flight to Dau Tieng. The plane was a C-7A transport and I sat up front with the pilots. Penny did the rounds, chatting to the soldiers sitting along the sides of the plane. Hanson just sat and sang to himself. We had to stick .302 bullets in our ears, which a soldier gave us, to lessen the noise from the engines. It was much easier to talk with bullets in our ears.

It was dark when we arrived at the camp and we offloaded and wandered off down the runway, following the soldiers.

We thumbed a lift in a jeep to Joe and Bill's company and took Hanson with us into the mess tent. As the company started to wander in for chow, we sat grinning at a table waiting for our men. Sure enough, they ambled in, filled their trays and turned and saw us. Grins broke out on their faces. We ate, catching up on each other's news, and then Penny, Hanson and I went over to the Division

Commander's office and reported in officially (for once). He frowned when he saw us, but couldn't fault our TDY orders. He knew something funny was going on, but just couldn't work it out. Silently, I thanked the terrible phone system, knowing he had Buckley's of ringing Saigon to check our credentials. Anyway, for once, mine were in order.

After an exhausting night in the VIP quarters with Hanson singing alone in his bunk (our noise didn't seem to worry him), the boys left by early light and we readied ourselves for the 8am 'Charlie Chopper' up onto Nui Ba Den.

At the last moment, Bill drove up to the helipad and asked Penny to stay the day with him. He figured she could keep out of the commander's way all day — I figured he had ideas of how to spend his day other than working. So Penny did not come up on the mountain with us. It was an extremely fortunate thing that she did not, if she had, she would have been caught out on her 'sickie' from the Saigon office and strongly reprimanded. The events that took place on the mountain had bad repercussions for Hanson and for me.

On the chopper ride up, which took only about 15 minutes, Hanson and I had a joint each. I was still convinced that the stuff had no effect on me whatsoever. The gunners on each door of the Huey chopper also begged a smoke and Hanson must have felt expansive by this stage, as he gave them both quite a supply from his little plastic bag.

With cameras slung around our shoulders, flash bags and clipboards, we stepped out on to the top of the mountain. The chopper was quickly divested of its supplies

— the PX goods we had come to see distributed and to photograph and get comments on from the guys — and it took off again without stopping its engines.

I looked around. We were standing on a raised flat piece of dirt lined with rocks around its edges to form a homemade helipad. We followed the soldiers carrying the boxes and crates down the side of the helipad into a large depression about 15 metres in diameter. Cut into the sides of the resultant hill were bunker openings, heavily sandbagged. We were welcomed by the company commander, a lieutenant named Cross. One fellow ran and hid in his bunker. He hadn't seen a girl for more than eight months, I was told, and he was overcome. The men were due for a Red Cross visit soon and were really looking forward to talking to the Donut Dollies, the American civilian girls who came to Vietnam for a couple of months at a time and did the rounds of the fire bases to keep up the morale of the troops. I figured I could keep my own morale up — I didn't need the Red Cross to sanction my activities.

Cross took us into the 'working' bunker, which was airconditioned. Apart from the military radio equipment, a bar was set up, a hexagonal green felt-covered card table and a small pool table were in the centre of the room, with stereo equipment in a corner. The guys had certainly tried to make their stay up on the mountain as comfortable as possible.

We had a drink while talking to Cross and some others. Hanson had a lemonade or something, while I had a bourbon. Neat and warm. By this time, Hanson was nearly zonked and I was getting giggly, so we figured we had better get our work done so we could enjoy the rest of the day. The crates had been ripped open by the guys outside and they were poring over magazines, candies, cameras, wristwatches, cigarettes and booze. One soldier was desperately trying to beat the others off the crates while he checked off his order form.

'Only guys who have orders,' he kept shouting. They all ignored him.

Hanson got some terrific photographs, ducking in and out of the group, clicking and flashing away. I started interviewing the fellows: 'How long since you've had any PX goods up here?' 'Where are you from; what's your name?' 'How long since you've seen a civilian?' 'Have you seen your newest PX catalogue?' And so on.

Half an hour of work and we were finished for the day. The chopper was due back at 4pm, so I joined a crap game going on in one of the bunkers, joint in one hand, bourbon in the other. I had won about $400 when the bloody Vietcong decided to launch an attack on the mountain.

First of all, the rockets whizzed overhead and landed well past our depression. Then their aim improved, and the rockets started to smash into the side of the hill near us. The empty crates were blown up where we had left them. I raced out and took photographs. Hanson got terribly excited and the two of us stood outside watching the camp spring into action, swinging machine guns around to face the enemy, lining up the 105mm Howitzers. I begged to be allowed to have a go on the guns and stood behind the big Howitzer and pulled the lanyard. Boom. I felt terrific. I don't imagine I hit anyone though.

Hanson shouted, 'Quick, Holly, stand up for a minute on the edge there and hold up this watch.' I thought, too, that this would be a terrific photo for the *Exchange Talk*. I could see the caption: DARING REPORTER GETS PX WATCH SUPPLY TO TROOPS UNDER FIRE …

I posed beautifully right on the rim of the depression, with my brightly coloured skirts blowing in the wind, watch held high in my hand. The shooting stopped momentarily. The Cong couldn't believe their eyes. I jumped down and the machine guns started up again. Laughing, Hanson and I courted death, popping our heads up over the edge to see the Cong below us down the hill.

We could see movement in the trees below, flashes of fire and our guys' tracers firing into the trees. We went back into the headquarters bunker and listened to the company commander ordering assistance from the 25th Infantry below us. Then the Cobra choppers came up from the plantation, firing rockets into the Cong positions. I was more scared of being hit by one of these than by the Vietcong, whose aim was notoriously bad.

A Cobra landed on the helipad and Cross pushed Hanson and me out, shouting, 'Get aboard, get off.' He had rung for a chopper to evacuate us, so we quickly rounded up our gear and leapt aboard. A gunner wrapped a flak jacket around me and indicated that I should also sit on one (ouch) and we took off smartly back towards the plantation.

Penny was there to meet us, jumping up and down in excitement. She was driving Bill's jeep. 'Come on,' she shouted. 'Come down to the perimeter and let's watch.'

We roared away from the helipad, into a far corner of the Michelin plantation grounds. The Cong were also firing on the division, so we sat behind the sandbags and watched the war going on. Hanson and I both took photographs again.

It was all over within 45 minutes. We headed up to the mess tent for lunch. I felt very blasé about the whole thing. We were real war veterans, Penny and me. We talked quite knowledgeably with the soldiers about what had happened. I couldn't wait to get back to Saigon to tell the other girls.

Our C-7A came for us mid-afternoon and we climbed aboard. Soon we were back at Tan San Nhut Airport, but we walked with a swagger as we got off the plane. Real war vets, we were.

'See,' said Hanson in his usual gloomy way, 'you didn't need a gun after all.'

The next morning in the office I realised that I would not be able to talk openly about the events on Nui Ba Dinh. There was a good chance that if the PIO Officer found out what happened, I wouldn't get any more travel duty. Hanson handed his reels of film over to Bernard Roblis, the photo developer, and we had to keep the photographs hidden until we had sorted out 'ours' from 'theirs'. Captain Morris was most anxious to see the results of our TDY and it was difficult to keep him out of the developing room until we had swiped all the negs of me standing on the rim under fire. Bernard did us some prints each, which we smuggled home.

I wish I had made sure he had handed all the prints over, because a few months later they became the most well-known photographs in the Vietnam Regional Exchange. And they cost me my job as a reporter.

Chapter Seven

OH GOODIE — MORE GIRLS

MY BIRTHDAY IN June came and went. Penny's birthday was the same date and Kerry organised a surprise party for us both at the Choi-oi Club. We had wandered upstairs after work for our usual Attitude Adjustment Hour and, as we opened the door, cries of 'Surprise, surprise' greeted us. We were both touched.

I treated myself to a 50cc Honda motorcycle for my birthday present. It cost $130 and came in a box. I had to put it together — screw on the handlebars and attach the wheels. I was thrilled with it, but *Papasan* saw me fiddling with it outside our house and muttered to himself. I think he was sorry I was now independent of his morning rides to work. Still, he had the other girls. I figured *Papasan* could retire on the tips we gave him for pedicab rides.

Just as I was finished assembling my bike, *Papasan* arrived with a can of fuel and we siphoned it into the tank. With instruction booklet in one hand and the entire neighbourhood of Vietnamese watching, I propped the Honda up on its stand and started the engine. It purred away and I was delighted, and threw away the book. I revved the hand accelerator, listening with joy to its roar. I decided then I had better give it a try (having never ridden a motorbike before). In Saigon, one didn't need a licence to ride a bike under 50cc (mine was actually 49cc) and kids from seven years up raced around the city on motorbikes. With the motor running, and with the bike perched up on its stand, I revved the engine to what I thought was a good take-off speed. Standing beside the bike, I kicked away the stand.

As the fast-spinning back wheel hit the ground the bike took off, with me still hanging desperately onto the handlebars. I was dragged along on my knees, out into the traffic and up the back of a little Renault taxi that unfortunately happened to be passing by. The bike wound up on the roof of the taxi and I wound up under the wheels of the taxi.

The neighbourhood had followed this scene with great delight. They were all standing around, laughing politely behind their hands. It was the most emotion I had seen Vietnamese display in public. *Mamasan* came running out, clucking and picked me up. I was badly damaged on the knees and elbows, blood dripping everywhere. I hobbled back indoors, Van running out to collect my Honda and to explain things to the rather stunned taxi driver.

For being the only VRE employee to have had an accident before actually getting on the Honda, I was awarded the Royal Order of the Training Wheels when the story became known at work the next day. The order was on the wall of the Choi-oi Club and was given 'to those compatriots who daily face the streets of Saigon fearlessly on a Honda'. I took the training wheels home and fitted them to my bike. I used them for a week until I had got my balance and my knees and elbows had healed.

One guy, Bud, had been awarded the Royal Order of the Training Wheels for a very unusual accident. He had been travelling along, bothering no one, but travelling too close to the barbed-wire coils that lined the streets. Those coils were miles long, twisting around compounds and US facilities to help prevent an attack by Cong. Unbeknownst to him, Bud's back footrest got hooked up in a coil and he just kept sailing along ... until the wire reached its full extent and then whipped back, snatching his bike out from under him.

'I was poised in midair in a riding position for a full minute,' he reckoned, 'before I fell flat on my ass.'

August came and the Vietcong were still hammering away at various outposts around the country, but this offensive was not nearly as bad as Tet '68. I figured they had lost a lot of support because of what they did at Hue.

The personnel officer had left for Sydney, loaded down with presents for our parents and phone numbers to be rung of friends we had forgotten to write to. It seemed that we Aussies had proved so successful that the PX had placed further ads in the *Sydney Morning Herald*, and Mr Fogerty, the Personnel Manager, was going off to interview and employ more of us. We were looking forward to seeing new faces and had already spread the word around our military party friends that there would be more girls soon.

I had received a letter from an Australian officer friend from my Sydney days, Captain Ralph White. The letter had been sent from Vietnam to my home in Sydney and redirected by my mother to me in Saigon. Ralph had no idea I was in the country. The letter was brief, simply saying that he was quite enjoying his war and that he had bought a present for me, which he would give me on his return. I decided to visit Ralph, but first I rang him.

The phone system was rotten. We had a cartoon in our office of a skeleton sitting at a desk holding a phone with cobwebs fanning from it, and the caption, which came from the mouthpiece, read, 'Hello, hello, hello. Your call is through now.' It was not exaggerated. To call Ralph at 1st Battalion, B Company, 1 RAR, I had to go through six independent exchanges. My motto — anything is possible – prevailed and, after calling the exchanges, Tiger, ARVN, Deer, Ebony, Emperor, then asking for Bravo Company, I finally was able to ask for Ralph.

Tiger was the US facilities exchange. ARVN was the Army of the Republic of Vietnam exchange, and was bloody difficult to get beyond, but I managed simply by repeating 'Deer, Deer, Deer' over and over until the operator understood and connected me. Deer was an American outpost, I don't know where, and the operator there wanted to chat to me. Finally, I got onto Ebony and an Aussie voice answered. Oh, he sounded good. Then to Emperor, part of the base at Nui Dat, then finally to Bravo Company.

'Bravo Company,' said a male Aussie voice.

'May I speak with Captain White please?' I inquired politely.

There was stunned silence.

'Hello, hello,' I said, 'Captain White, please.'

'Just a minute.'

I held on, hoping the line wouldn't be cut off.

'White speaking,' Ralph's voice came on.

'Hello Ralph, darling,' I said, 'It's me. Holly.'

'Shit.'

'What.'

'Where the hell are you?'

'In Saigon,' I answered, peeved that he didn't sound excited to hear from me.

'Well, for Christ's bloody sake,' he shouted, 'I'm in the middle of bloody battle here.'

He was speaking from one of those hand phones in a little pack on the back of a soldier.

'Can I come and visit you?' I asked.

'Hey, listen, Charlie is listening, so I can't give dates, but I'll ring you back just as soon as this fight is over and we'll make arrangements. OK?' he answered.

So I gave him my number and he hung up quickly. A pox on him, I thought.

He never did ring back. Probably found it impossible, being a mere male, to get through six exchanges. But he did come up to Saigon for a weekend with two of his mates and we all had a wow of a time. God, nine months in the country, and my first date with an Australian soldier — and an ex-lover from Sydney days. Maxim's of Paris had closed down by this stage, so we dined at the Mayfair, then all came back to our house where the boys bedded down on air mattresses on the floor and Ralph and I climbed into my bed. Sure enough, in the morning there was no one on the air mattresses. Lil and Penny had taken pity on the other two and invited them into their beds. The sad result was that Lil somehow got pregnant to one of them and had to be sent home a few months later. She complained bitterly.

'Fancy coming all this way and getting pregnant to a damn Aussie,' she stormed. 'I could have stayed home and done the same thing.'

I wangled a TDY to Vung Tau soon after this and visited the Australian base at Nui Dat. The Australians looked after Phuc Thuy Province, which was reputed to be the safest place in the country, so much so that those American military men who could not afford their R and R in Sydney or Hawaii or Tokyo went to the town of Vung Tau for a vacation by the seaside. The Australian base was well set up and included a full-size Olympic pool. The pool attendant, an enlisted draftee, told me, 'No one will believe what this daddy did in the war,' as he poured chlorine into the pool filter.

The town of Vung Tau was pretty and, as Vietnamese rarely swim, the beautiful beach was virtually untouched.

I was dying to have a swim, as I hadn't seen sand and surf for almost a year, but I found it impossible to purchase a swimsuit in the town. I resolved to always carry one with me from then on, as I missed out on a swim in the Aussie pool, too.

While I was there, several soldiers at Nui Dat approached me to get them American Coca-Cola from the PX on my ration card, so I went into Vung Tau and got three cases which I took back to the base. In return, I was given three cases of Victoria Bitter and, when I got back to Saigon, Penny went wild over the good ol' Aussie beer. We handed cans around the office, saying, 'Here, Yanks. Try some GOOD beer, not that piss you call beer.' The Americans really liked Aussie beer and offered to buy cases from me whenever I could get them. I was in the black market business from then on, in a small way. We used up every ration card we could beg, borrow or steal on cases of Coke, took them down to the Aussie PX at Free World Forces and swapped them for beer. Then we sold the beer to the Yanks at truly exorbitant prices. It helped pay the rent.

In mid-October, the next contingent of Australians arrived — a few men, but FIVE girls. Terrific. I made a point of being at the airport to greet each one, as they arrived on staggered flights. Justine Ellis and Trudi Yochuria arrived first. Justine was a small, pretty, brown-headed girl, and Trudi — poor Trudi — was an Australian-born Japanese with the broadest Australian accent imaginable, but she looked just like a Vietnamese. Her troubles started almost immediately she left the airport building. She was stopped twice on the way to the jeep by White Mice asking to see her ID card. They couldn't believe that she truly didn't speak Vietnamese and couldn't understand their questions. From then on, every time we took Trudi out in public we took Chantou, too, to translate and to explain. The first words we taught Trudi to say in Vietnamese were '*Toi la Uc Dau Loi*' — I'm an Australian.

Molly and Stephanie arrived next. Molly was a red-haired bitchy type and she went to work in the Security Section. She promptly moved in with the Chief of Security, a fat major, and eventually married him. They deserved each other. They never mixed with any of their workmates and just mooned around each other all day.

Stephanie was beautiful, naively sexy, a virgin and 27 years old. She was assigned to the Concessions Branch as a secretary and was in charge of about 30 Vietnamese employees. They loved her. She was gentle and understanding and prone to saying things to her long-suffering boss, Mr Karl, that were unintentionally vulgar. We had all learnt through experience not to call an eraser a 'rubber'. A rubber was a Tic 21 — Necessity Item. An eraser was what you rubbed out typing errors with. Steph was sitting at her typewriter one day, carefully erasing with a round blue typewriter eraser when she looked up at Mr Karl and said, 'Gee, you Americans have funny rubbers, you know. Ours are much better. They are long and pointed and have a little brush on the end.'

One evening, up at the Choi-oi Club, where we were having dinner, Kerry, Penny and I were talking to Steph about our love lives in the war zone. We were raving on a bit, telling her just how lovely every American was in bed, when Steph said quietly, 'I don't know what you are talking about. I've never even seen a man naked, let alone gone to bed with him.'

We were stunned. We had all presumed that Steph knew what we knew and a rather embarrassed silence ensued.

Penny, in her usual manner, waved her arms and said, 'Well, do you want to find out?'

Steph nodded shyly. I pulled out paper and pen from my clipboard and we drew drawings and diagrams, giving Steph her first lesson in the art.

Kerry couldn't believe that Steph was a virgin.

'No, really, how come you have never had a man?' she insisted.

'Where have you been? In a convent or something?'

'Yes,' said Steph. 'Until six months ago I was a nun.'

We shouted with laughter, until Steph convinced us she was telling the truth. So we got our heads together and planned Steph's initiation.

'It will have to be someone short,' said Kerry. 'First lovers are dangerous. We don't want her falling in love or anything like that.'

'And it will have to be someone kind and sensitive,' I volunteered. 'But who?'

Just then, a visiting colonel, Dave Byrnes, came to our table and joined us, and we eyed one another knowingly, nodding. Yes, Dave was the man. He was obviously quite taken with Stephanie, he was married, so that ended any romantic notions Steph might have afterwards, and he was a really neat, clean, presentable man.

We didn't have to do much, just fade away from Steph and Dave at the right moment, leaving nature to take its course. Dave, of course, asked Steph out to dinner the next night and, a few nights later, Steph, very nervous and dressed to kill, waited on the patio of the club for Dave to collect her after work.

'Tonight looks as if it's it,' she told us. 'Dave has invited me to his house for a private dinner — just the two of us.'

'Have you told him you're a virgin yet?' I asked her.

She shook her head dumbly. 'I don't quite know how to bring up the subject.'

'Well, good luck, kiddo,' we told her, and held her hand and fed her drinks until Dave arrived.

The next morning we rushed to the office to seek out Stephanie. 'How did it go? What happened? Tell us everything.'

'He was angry with me,' she told us, 'but I cried and then he really got tender and gentle, and we went to bed. It wasn't bad, but he says it gets better the more we practise.'

Steph and Dave practised nightly for weeks and Steph changed gradually into a self-confident woman. 'It's wonderful to throw off the shackles of my background,' she told me. 'I was raised in a Catholic orphanage and thought that I could get love and fulfilment as a nun, but I was wrong. Now I know what I want from life — a husband, children, a home.'

She was true to Dave until he left to go home to the States, and Dave, in turn, treated Steph with respect and kindness. He certainly spent his war fruitfully.

Steph shopped around carefully for her next lover. She came to parties up-country with us on choppers each Saturday night, but slept in VIP quarters until she met a doctor with nine months left in-country, stationed just 20km out from Saigon. They were a happy couple.

The last girl to arrive in-country from Sydney was Gail Williams. The moment we met Gail, we knew she was one of us. She was English by birth and had that wonderful Pommy humour — a sense of understatement. Her quips and cracks at the system and at the Americans kept us in constant laughter. We couldn't wait to turn her loose on the boys. She took Vietnam by storm — and the country, and us, were never the same again.

Chapter Eight

NEW YEAR AGAIN — SO SOON

I HAD BEEN trying desperately to get some home leave. Thirty days in Sydney would have suited me fine, but it was not to be. I was told that if I gained an exit visa from Vietnam, there was every possibility that I would not be granted a re-entry visa … and I certainly did not intend to leave the country permanently yet. So my dreams of Christmas at home with my family had to be forgotten.

Gail had moved in with Kerry, Penny and me, taking Lil's vacant bed. Like Scarlett O'Hara, Gail was not beautiful, but after two minutes in her company, every man was besotted. She had wit and charm, combined with extreme self-confidence. I heard that she was very, very good in bed.

Christmas was not a Vietnamese celebration, but we tried hard to make it so. A group of workers from the office organised toys and clothing to be sent from America by their families and we loaded up the big PX vehicle with sacks, and one of the men dressed up in a Santa suit. We drove to the local Catholic orphanage, Santa sweating profusely and nearly fainting from the heat. Arrangements had been made previously with the nuns and the little children had been told the story of Christmas. Even so, nearly every child was terrified of Santa, so, with great relief, Santa removed his suit and beard. I went along to take photographs for the newspaper and, for once Hanson showed some emotion when he saw children on crutches and some with limbs missing.

Vietnam was a Buddhist country and the French had tried to Christianise it, but failed. The Vietnamese figured that one god was good, two even better, and three or four would certainly ensure good fortune, so they practised Christianity by incorporating some of the Catholic ritual into their Buddhist ceremonies.

Part of the problem of the country at that time was that President Thieu was Catholic, his predecessor had been Catholic and the majority of the people were Buddhist. Officially, the only orphanages were government sponsored and were run by Catholic priests and nuns, so any little homeless Buddhist was placed in one of these orphanages and promptly labelled 'Catholic'. The very sad thing about this policy was that only Catholic families were allowed to adopt the children from these orphanages and, although a great number of Buddhist families applied for permission to adopt children, they were refused on the grounds that they

could not supply a good Catholic upbringing for the
'Catholic' orphan. The result was overcrowded orphanages
and empty Buddhist families.

One woman I knew, Madam Doan, had seven children
of her own, was very wealthy and had a large villa in Saigon
and several country properties. She had a heart of gold and
had applied several times to adopt a child or children. But,
being a good Buddhist, she had been refused. She told me she
would never understand Christianity. It preached love for all
men, but refused to give loving homes to little orphans.

The 12th Combat Aviation Battalion at Phu Loi was
having a Christmas party and the girls had all been invited,
but Gail and I decided to be adventurous and travel up to Da
Nang near the demilitarised zone (DMZ) and take pot luck.
We would stay in the town and, no doubt, do our good deed
for the week by helping the marines and air force guys up
there celebrate the festive season.

I was quite pleased to be getting out of Saigon. The
pre-monsoon season was stifling, the cockroaches at home
had given birth to thousands of little babies and we couldn't
walk through the house without crunching them underfoot.
The rats seemed to have multiplied also, so I figured that
it must be spring. Six-inch-long flying cockroaches made life
a little difficult, getting into our hair and food. Gail had a
swift, if dangerous, method of killing rats. She sat on her bed
and threw One-A-Day vitamin pills on the floor. The rats
couldn't resist this treat and, as they came within reach, she
smashed down across the middle of their backs with a piece

of rubber hose, killing them instantly. Rabies was prevalent and if one had jumped at her and bitten her, her chances of a horrible death were excellent.

So Gail and I packed our party dresses and thumbed a lift on a Hercules from Saigon to Da Nang. The pilots of the plane all recommended we stay at the Grand Hotel, Da Nang's best, so we got a lift to the hotel and walked into the foyer.

The hotel might have been grand once, but now it was old and seedy. A wide staircase ascended from the foyer to the floors above. We told the lady at the reception desk that we wanted a room for two for one night.

'Two thousand piastres with airconditioning,' she told us.

'How much without?' we inquired.

'Eighteen hundred.'

We figured it was worth the extra 200 piastres (about $20) to have airconditioning. We were hot, sticky and smelly. We paid the extra and a little man grabbed our bags and ran flat out up the stairs. We chased him, losing sight of him around corners. There were mangy dogs sitting in the hallways, who barked at us as we raced past. Finally, on the third floor of the hotel, we found the little man waiting outside a room. The room did not have a lock on the door; in fact, the doors were swinging bar doors. I was apprehensive about being unable to lock myself in, but he explained by hand expressions that none of the doors had locks. Still, we had brought nothing of value with us, so we indicated to him to show us in. We went through the swing doors into a hallway, off to the right of which was a very large tiled bathroom (no hot water). Beyond that was the bedroom, with two single wooden framed beds and no wardrobe, just one chest of drawers. Two long sash windows at the rear were curtained in flimsy material and, between the windows, was our blessed airconditioner. The man shooed two large moth-eaten dogs off the beds, plonked our bags on the floor and held out his hand for a tip, grinning at us. We gave him some money and told him to *di di*.

'Last one in the shower's a shit,' sang Gail, peeling off her dusty clothes.

'After me,' I yelled, stripping also.

Gail raced over to the airconditioner and turned it on full blast. 'A nice cold wash, then I'm going to lie naked on that bed in the cool air and die for another hour,' she said.

The bathroom was like a large shower recess, with a tap low to the floor, a hand shower above and the floor sloping away to a drain hole at the other end. There was no plug. We turned on both taps and took about half an hour washing our hair, rinsing underwear and getting cool. As I towelled myself dry I thought about the bedroom getting icy cold — lovely.

Chatting, we walked back into the bedroom. There was no noticeable difference in the temperature. In fact, it felt warmer now than before. We checked the airconditioner — it was blowing cold air out fast.

Then Gail looked more closely at the windows.

'The stinking little bastards,' she exclaimed. 'There's no bloody glass in the windows.'

For a moment, I was furious, thinking of the extra money we had paid for the room. But then we caught each other's eye and burst into laughter. Together we examined the airconditioner. Sure enough, it was an American brand, stolen from the PX store.

'Poor little Viets,' I cried. 'They are so unsophisticated and gullible. Someone told them they could charge more for their rooms if they had airconditioners in them and the poor buggers probably paid a fortune to buy conditioners on the black market.'

'And forgot to tell them to put glass in the windows or they wouldn't work!' finished Gail. 'But isn't that just typical of this whole bloody war?'

It was. The Vietnamese so envied the American soldier and his buying power that they would do practically anything to have what *he* had, to the extent of buying expensive electronic equipment without having a clue of how to use it. It was a real peasant mentality. I was pleased that at least a certain number of Vietnamese — those who worked for the Americans in various jobs — would glean a little knowledge of the modern way of life, but here at Da Nang, in the boondocks, civilisation only went as far as owning the item, not knowing how to work it.

'Well, lady,' I said to Gail, 'if we're going out to find ourselves some entertainment, we had better get started.'

We dressed and, locking our bags and shoving them under the beds, we set off towards a Chinese restaurant on the river's edge that had been recommended by the receptionist at the hotel. We were wandering along the path by the river when a voice hailed us.

'Holly, Gail.'

It was Don Freeman, a lover of Gail's from Saigon, who had been transferred to Da Nang earlier that month. We were pleased to see him and he joined us for lunch at the restaurant. Afterwards, he took us to the White Elephant Club in the town, where he made a big hit entering with two girls on his arm. In no time at all, it was agreed between us and his friends at the club that we should be smuggled into the air base, so the guys set about buying local food for a party.

We drove across the bridge and Don pointed out the sunken ships in the harbour. He also pointed out the *Helgaland*, a Swedish hospital ship that treated civilians only, be they Viet Cong, ordinary Vietnamese or even Australians.

'We always know when we are going to be attacked,' Don told us, 'because the *Helgaland* ups anchor and leaves the port. The Cong tell the hospital ship to leave, and then, when all the fighting is over, the ship comes back into port and the Cong take their wounded on board to be treated.'

When we arrived at the gates of the air base, Don introduced us to the soldiers on guard and we told them our usual story of being reporters on official duty. I had typed and signed our travel orders and we showed these to the guards, who waved us on.

At Don's squadron mess, we pulled stools up to the bar and ordered drinks. As the other pilots started wandering in, they gathered around us, eager to hear our voices and to talk about Saigon and Sydney, both of which many of them had visited.

Behind the bar was a garbage chute down which the empty cans were put. A game that the pilots had was to stand up on the rung of the stool, lean across the bar and throw the can into the chute. If you missed, you had to buy a round.

That afternoon cost me a fortune in drinks. The more I drank, the worse my aim. Gail, on the other hand, became most proficient, standing on her stool and screeching 'Yahoo, bombs away' with each throw. The guys started laying bets on her aim. Someone pulled out a set of dice and, as night fell, we were wholly engrossed in gambling. The only round of drinks Gail had to buy was when she fell backwards off her stool. She insisted her bottom hadn't left the seat — and, to me, it looked as though it hadn't — but the boys said it wasn't counted. As she fell, she had a drink in her hand and she didn't spill a drop. So they said that counted for something and bought her a bottle of Scotch.

On the enclosed patio outside the bar, trestle tables were set up and loaded with good food. We filled our plates and sat down on the grass, bantering with the pilots.

The fellows had all dug into their care packages from home and the tables were filled with homemade cookies and jars of nuts and candied fruit. We blew up balloons and someone even produced a small plastic tree with a star on top. Someone else brought out a Christmas cake his mum had sent.

'Happy Christmas,' we said to each other and the entire squadron lined up for a kiss from the girls. The nurses who had joined the party were a good natured lot and we kissed all the boys, in good fun, awarding points for the best kisser.

The jollity went on into the early hours of the morning. I waited up to see Santa come. Gail and Don disappeared. There was a jam session going on in another mess hall, so we walked towards the sound of the music.

A Filipino band was on the stage, beating out really good dance music for the airmen and officers.

By popular demand, the 'theme song' of the war was played again and again, the guys all shouting 'more' whenever the band tried to stop.

'We gotta get outta this place,' they sang, beating beer cans to the rhythm, 'if it's the last thing we ever do. We gotta get outta this place, girl, there's a better life for me and you.'

Hey Jude was another favourite and ensured a 10-minute dance whenever it started up. *I'm Leaving on a Jet Plane* made a lot of fellows morose and homesick. But the band played on.

The next morning, we had Bloody Marys for breakfast with our powdered eggs. Gail turned up and ate like a horse. The Lady is a Tramp. Then Don drove us back across the bridge to the hotel. I noticed that the *Helgaland* was still in port. We collected our bags, which incredibly were still where we had left them, showered (Gail and Don together to save water) and then Don drove us out to the airport and saw us onto the C-130 for Saigon. Gail now had his address and phone number and promised to write to him in-country.

Back home again, we swapped stories with Kerry and Penny, and exchanged gifts. Trying to shop for special gifts in Saigon was hopeless and none of us had wanted to buy anything we could get for ourselves in the PX. Kerry, bless her, gave me her favourite party dress, which I always wanted to borrow. Penny gave me a rear-vision mirror for my Honda and Gail gave me a dozen reels of film. I gave each of the girls some Montagnard crafts I had purchased on a trip to Dalat.

Our Green Beret friends knocked on our door during the afternoon with a case of steaks and they stayed on for dinner.

Mamasan and Van cooked for us and took their own steaks upstairs. They quite approved of our food-carrying fellows, as we always gave them a good supply of whatever we were given.

Boxing Day was not a holiday, so we had to go back to work. The Black Cats from Phu Loi had given messages to the girls for Gail and me that they would not tolerate our missing the New Year party they had planned. So, with a great feeling of nostalgia and deja vu, I rode out to Tan San Nhut Airport, around the back to the waiting Chinook and climbed aboard for my second New Year's Eve in Vietnam.

It had been a while since I had been to my favourite party place and many of the faces had changed. Some new ones looked promising, though. The camp doctor, Captain

Frank M. Washington ('Just call me Doc') was simply beautiful and Penny latched onto him immediately. There was a funny little fellow there, a chopper gunner called Jimmie, and Trudie found a soul mate in him. They were both about the same size. Carmen, of course, hooked her arm possessively through the battalion commander's arm and that was the last we saw of her for the night. It also got the top brass out of the way for us all to let our hair down in proper style. Good old Carmen.

Chantou made off with the chef and was last seen telling him what she wanted to take back to Saigon with her as he rifled through his freezer and cupboards. Steph came up, bringing a friend from Saigon with her, a top-ranking naval officer who wore civvies so that he didn't have to explain his presence to anyone. Kerry, Justine, Gail and I all mixed freely, dancing with everyone in turn.

When it grew dark, we raced outside to the pool, stripping as we ran. Skinny-dipping is fun at any time, but at night, in a semi-lit pool in the middle of a war, with rockets sounding off and flashing in the distance — just four girls and 100 men — it was delicious. Slippery hands grabbed at our legs, we were dragged under the water and kissed by anonymous lips. Fellows on the poolside souvenired our clothing, but we were beyond caring. We swam, raced, jumped out and dived back in. Tantalising and elusive. The flares lit up the sky momentarily, bathing our bodies in a weird yellow light. The chaplain, not the bald-headed guy in the green suit of a year ago, appointed himself our guardian angel and fetched towels and sets of fatigues for us to wear when we got out of the pool.

'You girls will be the death of me,' he complained. 'When you lot arrive, I never get anyone to chapel on Sunday mornings.'

We promised him that the next Sunday we spent at Phu Loi he could advertise his service with 'girls will be present', thus ensuring a good congregation. He was mollified as we assured him earnestly that we would come to chapel at the very next opportunity.

'The men hang around the mess hall waiting for you girls to emerge on Sunday mornings and won't go to chapel in case they miss seeing you,' he told us.

New Year was rung in in proper style, kisses all round. Kerry missed the Wyoming time call because she had toddled off with someone. Justine, Gail and I went through the tearful, hugging, hand-holding nostalgia at the Sydney time call, then departed to bed with our chosen gentlemen.

The next day was a working day for us all. The uncivilised Yanks didn't treat New Year's Day as a holiday, so a chopper was organised for us at 6am to take us back to Saigon in time for work. As I sat in the chopper, cold in the misty morning air, tired, hungover and waiting for the other girls to be rounded up and brought to the helipad, I wondered what the war was all about. In the past year, I had hardly seen any real action. I supposed I had expected 'war' to be like it was portrayed in the movies, all guns and fighting and tough-talking men. But it wasn't like that at all.

Sure, I had seen action, but it was a very minor part of the war. Even the fellows whose parties we attended at weekends, and whom we met in Saigon, hadn't really seen an enemy face to face. We saw *evidence* of enemy activity, but never the actual enemy.

I estimate that 80 per cent of soldiers who spent their 12 months in Vietnam never saw any fighting. Doc Washington had told me, when we were discussing war injuries, that two-thirds of the injuries he treated were self-inflicted: accidents with guns, barroom brawls that ended in a shoot-out, drunken driving, people burned from smoking near ammo and petrol dumps. One colonel, he told me, received a Purple Heart because, as some rockets started coming into the base one night, the phone rang and the colonel ran to answer it, hand outstretched. He hit a pencil with his middle finger, the lead sliding up under the nail, which later became infected. 'The colonel insisted on being awarded the Purple Heart,' Doc said, 'because he was, in fact, "wounded as a result of hostile action". But they had to make up some story for his citation that looked better than being attacked by a pencil.' I wondered how many guys would go home and tell their wives and families the truth about the war.

Back in Saigon at work, I was called into the commander's office. He had been given the photographs Hanson and I took at Nui Ba Den, particularly the one of me standing waving a wristwatch as the bullets flashed past.

'This will not do, Holly,' he said unhappily. 'I have been asked to send you home.'

I cried on his shoulder and begged not to be sent home in disgrace. I promised to be a good girl and not do anything so foolish again. He softened a little and then said he would look at the Manning Document and see if he could transfer me to a desk job ... but my days as a reporter were over.

Sadly, I went back downstairs. Captain Morris had been told I was to have no more TDY and was sympathetic.

'Holly, my girl,' he explained, 'we just can't afford to have you shot.'

So, with heavy heart, I waited to be told what my next assignment would be.

Chapter Nine
TET 1969

ON 10 FEBRUARY, the Cholon PX was sabotaged. Fires broke out and badly damaged the store and quite a bit of stock. I had become complacent during the peaceful time since the previous November and had almost forgotten that a war was going on. But the fire brought home the reality of my situation again and was a warning of the proximity of Tet. Within the next two days, I witnessed a gunfight in the street outside my house between what looked like a 12-year-old-boy and an ARVN soldier. Several shots were fired and the soldier was shot dead. Two American soldiers were blown up in their jeep in the middle of downtown Saigon. The jeep had been booby-trapped while the soldiers were off sightseeing. We were all warned officially not to mingle in crowds and to stay away from public facilities. Yet another post office was blown up.

The VRE headquarters in Cholon was sandbagged heavily and rolls of barbed wire pulled across the street around the entrance. The guards in the pillbox at the front

became very conscientious for once and thoroughly checked
IDs and we had to open our handbags to be searched each
time we entered the building. We were told that a shuttle bus
with armed guards would collect us each morning for work
during Tet and would deliver us home at night. Beyond that,
we were not to set foot on the streets. I took this advice very
seriously and we advised Gail, who had not been in-country
for the celebration of Tet 1968, to take heed also. The entire
Schwartz family, including Kerry, packed up and went to
Bangkok for the holiday period.

Colonel Verona had finished his job in Vietnam and
had returned to the US, 'the land of the Big PX', as he called
it. He was replaced by Colonel Newman, who, if anything,
was even sweeter than Colonel Verona. It was Colonel
Newman who made the decision about my next posting and
he called me to his office to tell me.

'Well, my little Aussie,' he started, smiling, 'I reckon
I've found a slot for you that will keep you out of trouble.'

I was to be sent to Cam Ranh Bay, the largest port on
the mid-coast of the country. My job was to be the Assistant
Civilian Personnel Officer for the entire Second Corps. It
was a two-grade promotion on my present job. I was quite
pleased about the new job, but terribly unhappy about
leaving Saigon and my hootch-mates, Kerry, Penny and Gail.

When I told them of my posting, Penny said, 'Don't
worry, we'll be up every weekend or so to see you, and you'll
still get down to Saigon, and we'll ring you every day,
so you'll hardly notice you've gone.'

I felt a bit better when I realised that friendship stretched across the miles, but Gail really showed me the brighter side of my posting.

'Your job up there is to organise the place into another Phu Loi and Dau Tieng. Check out the talent, line up the top brass, get the place in the palm of your hand and then send for us for the first party.'

'Done,' I laughed and, from then on, I had only twinges of sadness about leaving Saigon. I started to look forward to a new place and new faces.

I had been told I was to report to the Commander, Cam Ranh Bay Area Exchange, in late March. We girls had been invited to a 12th Combat Aviation Battalion party to celebrate George Washington's birthday on 22 February, and I realised that this would probably be my last Black Cat party. Carmen decided that it was to be the party to end all parties and she made an overnight trip to Phu Loi in the middle of Tet to organise the party with the company commander (that was her excuse anyway).

She came back to Saigon and told us of her plans. We made a shopping trip downtown and purchased yards of different coloured tulle. Kerry, a petite blonde, chose palest pink; Penny had aqua with silver flecks through it; Gail, a redhead at that time, chose bright emerald green; mousy Justine had black tulle. I chose electric blue with black thread woven through. Trudi and Chantou, both with long black hair, chose red and lemon respectively. We looked like a Puerto Rican wedding party.

The only purchase Carmen made was a 60cm-long ivory cigarette holder.

The boys at Phu Loi advertised the party around the camp and at the Saigon embassies with flyers pinned on mess hall doors, noticeboards and in bars:

THE BLACK CATS PRESENT
MONTE CARLO NIGHT!
Blackjack, roulette, poker, craps,
all gambling facilities
FINE FOOD $1   DRINKS 15c
Live Band — 'The Young Five'
YES, FOR YOUR COMFORT WE HAVE LADIES COMING

Their objective was to raise at least $600 to cement around the pool area and to install outdoor barbecue facilities at the pool. We girls were to be casino girls for the night and were to dress in costume for the occasion.

When we arrived by chopper that evening, we hustled into the VIP hootch and unpacked our bags. Each of us, except Carmen, first dressed in a bikini. Then, with needles and thread, we wound the tulle around out bodices and hips, gathering it into big bunches behind, which were stitched into place. The result was a rather slinky looking, leggy front view and a bustle and train effect from the rear. We thought we looked gorgeous. Carmen dressed herself in a long clinging black silk dress, pulled on long gloves and lit a cigarette in her ivory holder.

Thus arrayed, and to a fanfare from the band, we made our entrance into the Officers' Club to a standing ovation from the boys. Carmen marched in first, brandishing her cigarette holder and looking every bit the Madam. We trotted in after her and took our places behind the tables to assist in the running of the gambling. Gail joined a poker table, which until then, had had only two guys playing at it. Within minutes it was crammed full. Justine and Trudi played roulette, the crowd around that table thickening by the minute as more fellows from other companies and battalions heard about the casino girls. I dealt blackjack.

An hour later, Carmen whispered in my ear, 'Keep it going. We've collected well over $600 and the night is still young.' So we gambled, dealt cards, shook and threw dice, and kept the fellows spending money.

About midnight, I took a breather and went into the annex for some supper and dancing. The band had arrived at 10pm and some of the girls had been dancing, then bringing their partners back to the gambling. The night was a huge financial success.

I saw the chaplain throwing dice and went over to remind him that we had not forgotten our promise to attend chapel the next morning. He was pleased.

'I've already put a notice on the board to that effect,' he said. 'Gee, you girls have more power in this place than God.'

About 2am, I peeled off my casino outfit and danced barefoot in my bikini. Cheers went up from the crowd and the other girls followed suit. We all raced to the pool. I had met a rather sweet, shy fellow from Kansas, all Mom's apple pie and dimples, named Dale. We started kissing and fooling around in a dark corner of the pool, then, dripping wet, and still clutching each other, we walked across the compound to his room.

The compound was a large dirt square at the corners of which were sandbagged, underground bunkers. Dale's hootch was in the middle of a row of rooms lining one side of the compound. We went in, stripped and towelled each other dry. We fell on his army cot and started making fierce love to each other. He was beautiful. We had a shower together, a drink and then fell back on the cot again, this time for a lovely, long, slow one.

At 4.30am, the Red Alert siren went. We stopped, laughed at the inopportune timing of the Vietcong and then continued what we were doing. The door burst open and a soldier ran in shouting.

'We're being overrun. Take cover. The perimeter has been breached.'

I jumped up, my whole body trembling. I grabbed my wet bikini and tried to get into it but couldn't. Precious time was passing. Dale had slipped into his shorts and shouted at me, 'Get to the damn bunker, don't worry about THAT', indicating my attempts to dress.

I still hesitated, but Dale ran to the door, looked quickly up and down and then shoved me, stark bloody naked, out into the compound.

Just then, a 122mm rocket landed right behind Dale's wooden hootch. The blast of the explosion threw us both out into the dirt. Bits of wood and metal smashed into our bodies. We leapt up and ran flat out to the bunker entrance. Men were running everywhere, emptying the hootches and charging to the bunkers, guns at the ready. As I ran to the bunker, diagonally across the compound, I turned my head to look behind because I was expecting a bullet in the back at any moment. Behind me was a mob of men, all grinning and bypassing other bunkers to follow me. Christ, we had the most crowded bunker at Phu Loi that night.

I raced down the wide steps and, ignoring the surprised faces and lewd comments, crawled as far as I could into the dark third 'room' of the bunker. The chaplain was there and he swiftly removed his jacket and wrapped it around me. I was too frightened to cry.

The chaplain noticed blood running down my legs and became terribly concerned, so he cleared some guys off the bench and with not much privacy, I lay on my stomach while the chaplain examined my wounds. I had a bloody great wedge of wood stuck in my buttock, lots of splinters in my back, my knees and elbows were skinned badly (again!) and I had what looked like peppers of shrapnel in my thighs and behind my knees. I was a mess.

Dale was in a similar plight and the two of us lay face-down while the first aid sergeant patched us up. 'Holly's ass will need stitching,' he told the chaplain, 'so as soon as it's safe, get her over to the medical tent.'

Carmen arrived in the bunker, walking leisurely as if nothing unusual was happening. With great aplomb, and still in her long black evening gown, she marched through the bunker with an electric fan under one arm and a flask of hot coffee under the other. She had obviously been under fire before and knew how to make herself comfortable while waiting for the All Clear. She set up her fan, sharing it with Dale and me, and swigged at her flask. She told me that she had been under fire in the Philippines during World War II, and was quite used to spending time in a bunker. She then promptly curled up on the floor and went to sleep.

There was a telephone handset in the bunker and it flashed a light instead of ringing. The chaplain picked it up and listened. He said nothing. Then he replaced the handpiece.

'You three there, and you, and you,' he said, pointing to some men, 'to your posts now.'

The men got up, checked their ammo and, with pistols cocked, went quietly up the bunker stairs.

This procedure was repeated time and again, until only a few of us were left in the bunker. We could hear gunfire above us and footsteps thudding across the ground over our heads. Two soldiers with M16 rifles at the ready sat either side of the foot of the bunker steps. I had been given a .45 pistol, loaded and cocked, and a very lethal-looking knife.

'If you see legs in black satin trousers coming down those steps,' I was told, 'shoot first and ask questions later.' I did not shift my eyes from the steps from then on.

Six hours later it was all over and the All Clear siren was sounded. 'So much for my big Sunday service,' groaned the chaplain. 'I often wonder whose side He's on.'

Carmen, Dale, the chaplain and I emerged cautiously from the bunker, blinking in the bright sunlight. We made our way to the medical tent, only to find that Doc was at a conference at Vung Tau. There were a lot of wounded men lining up for medical attention. Carmen, in her forthright way, took stock of the situation and said to us, 'Well, don't just stand there. Hand me those swabs and that hypodermic.' She busied herself attending to wounds. The chaplain and I tried to patch up a very badly burned young man, whose skin was peeling from his arms and chest. He groaned and was delirious. Carmen gave him a shot of morphine and ordered a less badly wounded man to organise a medivac chopper to take the man to hospital in Saigon. We put him on a stretcher, placed sterile gauze over the salve we had applied and he was taken quickly to the waiting chopper.

For several hours Carmen, the chaplain and I worked hard, giving shots, stitching (my own bottom included) and cleaning wounds. When the last man had been treated and sent away, we meandered over to the mess tent and rounded up the chef for a meal of bacon and eggs and lots of strong, brandy-laced coffee.

The other girls had been told by this time that I had been wounded and, as I hobbled off to find them, swathed in bandages and looking very much the wounded soldier, all the men standing around outside raised a cheer.

We collected our gear and, by 4pm, were all on a Huey chopper back to Saigon. Our pilot chose to land at the helipad behind Third Field Hospital, as Tan San Nhut

Airport was still under Red Alert. The attack on Phu Loi had been just one of many offensives launched simultaneously on other bases. I heard later that most major bases had been attacked.

On 17 March, the Phu Loi chaplain came into my office. I was very surprised to see him.

'Ask your boss for a couple of hours off,' he said. 'You're coming with me right now. I have a chopper waiting at Free World Forces helipad.'

Permission granted, I rode up to Phu Loi with the chaplain, still mystified and a little worried because I thought I was in trouble again. The chaplain patted my hand and assured me that everything was OK.

We landed and drove to battalion headquarters where, before the entire company and on a raised platform, the commander presented me with a medal — the Purple Heart. The citation read, 'For being wounded as a result of a hostile action, not in participation in aerial flight, and also for being such a good soldier under extremely trying conditions.'

I didn't know what to say, apart from thank you. The assembly cheered and sang *For She's a Jolly Good Fellow*. Then I was rushed back to the chopper and flown home to Saigon, clutching my precious medal.

When I displayed the medal to all and sundry at VRE headquarters, many of the desk-soldiers were jealous. One man, carefully reading my citation, told me, 'You know it's not official?'

I knew it wasn't. And I didn't give a shit!

Chapter Ten

CAM RANH BAY, HERE I COME

FOR MY LAST night in Saigon, we decided we would celebrate with a girls' night out. We promised each other that no matter what irresistible man tried to move in on us, we would stick together and not be deterred from our intentions.

Work ceased in the information office at four in the afternoon. Vietnamese food, hot and garlicky, was laid out on the desks and my farewell office party got under way quickly. It was Saturday, and my plane was to leave Tan San Nhut about midday on Sunday, so I figured that my remaining hours left in Saigon were for fun.

As the office party wound down, my friends shepherded me out of the door and into a waiting jeep. Penny had borrowed the jeep from our Green Beret friends, promising to return it on Sunday. It was a hilarious trip downtown, mostly on the wrong side of the road, Penny feeling my leg for the gearshift with each change. None of us, except Kerry, was accustomed to driving on the wrong side of the road the American way. We tooted to soldiers in the street, hanging out of the jeep and blowing kisses.

Outside the Mayfair Restaurant, Penny conscientiously wrapped a chain around the steering column of the jeep, padlocked it and dropped the key down her bra. We paid a little Viet boy to watch the jeep for us and all moved into the restaurant.

There were nine of us — Penny, Carmen, Kerry, Justine, Gail, Trudi, Chantou, Marie and myself. Four Australians, one Yank, two Filipinas and a Vietnamese. Trudi didn't know what she was! Japanese, Australian or just plain TCN.

We all ordered French onion soup, then the chef came to our table to discuss the menu with us. On his advice, we ordered pork loin, coq au vin, chicken stuffed with aromatic herbs and basted in honey (a Viet dish); a variety of vegetable dishes, all superbly cooked, and many bottles of French champagne, which was prohibited by the Viet Government, so we had to pay black market prices for it. We finished with crepes suzette, cooked at the table, which was almost a floor show. Two GIs tried to butt in on us despite our protests. One became most abusive and sullenly called us 'officer material' and 'snobs'.

'Too bloody right, mate,' rejoined Gail. 'Officers know how to treat a lady, and you obviously don't. So just fuck off.'

Several officers eating nearby watched this little scene and one made a move to assist us, but I waved him off. Gail could handle anything.

The GI muttered something about all he could get were gooks, to which I took great offence. Chantou stood up, walked around the table and pushed her face right into his.

'I'm a gook,' she said through clenched teeth, 'and, no sweat, GI, I wouldn't be seen dead with the likes of you.'

We all clapped. Chantou resumed her seat and went on eating her crepes as though nothing had happened. The GIs grabbed their caps and left.

The meal cost close to $900. Oh well, that was the price we paid for black market goods. But it was worth it.

In a high mood, we discussed our next move.

'I want to see a Saigon tea bar,' I said. 'You know, the ones with Saigon Tea girls in them.'

Chantou said she knew of one a block away, so we followed her. We climbed the narrow stairs singly and Gail was the first to enter the bar, the rest of us loitering and gossiping behind her.

As she stepped into the bar, the band stopped playing and everyone in the room turned to stare at her. GIs with little Viet girls perched on their knees all looked at her curiously. Gail just stood there and looked back. An American voice from across the room drawled loudly, 'What's a nice girl like you doing in a clip joint like this?' And all the men laughed. They all looked drunk and dirty and unkempt, not at all like the men we were used to being seen with. Kerry whispered to me, 'God, the place is full of grunts.' The Vietnamese girls all glared at us, probably thinking we were going to try to take their customers from them. 'No sweat, girls,' I thought to myself. 'They're all yours.'

We pulled a couple of tables together and ordered Saigon tea, much to the surprise of the waitress. I had heard a lot about the bar girls, or B-girls, as they were known. They were usually refugee country girls with no way of earning enough money to feed themselves in the big city other than by perching on a bar stool next to a GI and letting him buy her drinks. Whether or not they ever sold anything more than their drinking company, I do not know, although Chantou insisted that they did. I really felt sorry for my fellow females and wondered how I would cope if my country was ever occupied by a foreign army.

'Don't ever worry about that,' said Gail when I mentioned this to her. 'You'll probably find that half the army is made up of our ex-lovers. We'd manage OK.'

The waitress argued that we shouldn't buy Saigon tea. 'Saigon tea cost many, many P [piastres],' she told us.

'How much?'

'Two hundred P.'

It was a high price for a cocktail glass of cold tea, but we were determined to try it. The Vietnamese rarely drank alcoholic beverages and thought it rather weird that we could spend an entire evening drinking as a form of entertainment. I wanted to see if I could spend an evening drinking Saigon tea as a living, as these girls did. One taste convinced me that I couldn't. It was watery, flat and tasteless. I pushed my glass aside and ordered a bourbon. It cost 500 P

— about $5. A GI could go through his entire salary in one night at these prices, I thought.

When we left the bar, we headed towards the I-House to see if we could talk our way past the doorman. Penny started to whistle the tune of *The Green Berets*. As she whistled, words came into my head and I stopped and gathered the girls around. We squatted on the pavement, Viet fashion, in a circle, and nutted out the words of what we called *The Saigon Tea Song*. It went to the tune of *The Green Berets* and was sung in a high squeaky voice that we thought sounded like a Vietnamese girl. Chantou supplied us with phonetical training on the first line of the song — '*Em yew anh nhew lan*', which means 'I love you too much'. We knew phrases such as '*di di mau*' (nick off quick), '*one beaucoup P*' (many piastres), and '*dien-ka-dow*' (crazy) and we put together a song that eventually became well-known across the country in various forms:

The Saigon Tea Song

Em yew anh nhew lam, Yankee
You come o' here and sit by me
You can buy me Saigon Tea
Maybe happen you sleep wit' me
We go your house, we take-a taxee
You want massagee, I give for free
But before you sleep wit' me
I say to you, 'one beaucoup P'
I go to sleep, I dream o' my house

And in the morning I quiet as mouse
I never know you dien-ka-dow
You say to me, 'you di di mau'
You Yankee, are Cheap Charlie
Now I know I no get P
You get screwed, you Numbah Ten
I never sleep wit' you again
Choi-oi!

We linked arms and, singing at the tops of our voices, marched along the pavement to the I-House. Of course we weren't allowed in — the doorman took one look at Trudi, Chantou, Carmen and Marie and shook his head. So we stood outside and threw rocks up at the front bay window, yelling 'We want Mario, we want Mario' until a very embarrassed Mario came down the stairs.

We told him about our song and he rushed back up to the bar to get paper, pen and his Spanish guitar. He told his boss he was going out for a break and joined us again downstairs. We moved down the street to the central square and, with Mario sitting on the wall of the fountain and the girls grouped around his feet on the grass, we treated Saigon to the first proper rendition of its own *Saigon Tea Song*. Passers-by stopped and listened, soldiers begged us for the words to the song, and we spent the time until curfew teaching it to all and sundry. Mario went back to the I-House and, we heard later, immediately sang it in the bar. It was an instant success.

At 10pm, curfew time, the streets became vacant as if by magic and we walked slowly back to the jeep. It wasn't there. 'Doesn't matter,' said Penny, feeling around inside the front of her dress, 'I've lost the key anyway, so we couldn't have driven home.'

We walked back to the main square and, just for the sheer hell of it, all had a swim in the fountain. Our peels of laughter brought the MPs running and, consequently, we were driven to our various homes in a paddy wagon.

The next day, the girls from my hootch came out to the airport with me and waved frantically as my C-130 took off. I watched them grow smaller as the plane circled higher and I cried. But only for a minute. There were too many lovely men on the plane for me to stay sad for long.

I had visited Cam Ranh Bay (CRB) as a reporter and knew a little of the layout of the base. It was a large island only 275 metres from the mainland village of Dong Ba Thin. On the mainland was a fenced-in checkpoint where everyone crossing the bridge to the island was signed in and out. There were three main facilities on the island, beside the big port facilities. To the left at the end of the bridge was the air base, home of the 12th Tactical Fighter Wing, the Phantom Jet pilots, the air force hospital, support planes and transport planes. It was there that I landed, on the huge airstrip. It was also where about one-third of the troops entering Vietnam landed in the big C-141 transport planes that brought them from America. Later on, just for fun on Sundays sometimes, I used to go out to the 22nd Replacement Battalion just to watch the faces of the newest arrivals.

To the right of the bridge and about 8km down a road that wound around by the water was the army base. This was where I was to be quartered and stationed. It was situated, in the usual army fuck-up style, right in the depression formed by a circle of large sand hills, which the tropical sun turned into a shimmering crater each day. The army also never bothered to connect septic tanks or a sewerage system to its base.

On the crest of the far sand hill, just high enough above the crater to get sea breezes from the other side of the island, was the Mini Court, a wired-in enclosure containing a dozen three-bedroom trailers for the exclusive use of colonels and generals. One trailer contained three Red Cross girls, who stayed three months at a time, and my trailer, B6, housed a female army officer, the Special Services librarian (an American), and now, me. The septic tank was connected on the hill and behind the Mini Court was the White House, the VIP quarters at which President Johnson stayed when he visited CRB.

Nearby was Tiger Lake, which was large enough for boating activities. I was pleased to discover that our Sydney sailing club, the Double Bay Eighteen Footer Club, had donated two yachts. I had done some sailing in Sydney and looked forward to some sport.

A dirt track wound over the hills and down to the very end of the island to the beautiful South China Sea coast. At the end of the road was Market Time, the naval base and home of the Seabees. To me it was like something out of Michener's *South Pacific*, or, when I got to know what went on down there, more like *McHale's Navy*: palm trees, powder fine sand, snack bars and clubs all along the beach. I was to spend a great deal of time at Market Time.

Assigned to Market Time by the PX and in charge of running the snack bar was an Australian man with whom I was to become lifelong friends. His name was Jeff Brandt and he had organised his Vietnamese staff so well that he could spend all day just lying on the beach with his transistor radio, socialising in the various club bars and gambling with the chief petty officers when he regularly relieved them of their pay cheques.

'Delegation is the word in this place,' he told me when I asked him how he did it. 'Train a good Vietnamese and pay her a little on the side and she will be worth her weight in gold to you.'

Jeff certainly lorded it over his staff, like a cocky little rooster. He would casually walk into the snack bar to check how things were going, or to count the takings, and he would growl at his girls. They all loved him, all took him with a grain of salt. They knew he had no bite. 'Mitter Jeff, Mitter Jeff,' they would call to him, 'I bin good girl, no give free hamburger to boyfriend today.' If he looked a little hungover, the Viet girls would fight over who would give him a neck massage. Jeff certainly had a nice war, even to the point of having his breakfast delivered to him in bed each morning by a doting Vietnamese staff member.

I settled myself into my new quarters, visiting the quartermaster to get my issue of mattress, cot, sheets and pillows. My room in the trailer was tiny, with room enough just for my cot and an electric fan on the floor. There were built-in wardrobes and a dressing table. It was stuffy and hot, as the effects of the airconditioner in the living room didn't reach beyond the hallway. But there was hot water laid on, a luxury I really appreciated, a full-length bath and a flush toilet that worked most of the time.

The kitchen, which was at one end of the living room, had a four-burner Protagas stove, coloured aqua, a matching refrigerator, and a double sink. I was in heaven after my hootch in Saigon. There were four telephones, one in each bedroom, and one in the living room.

Under the trailer lived large iguanas, which appeared regularly for scraps of food. There was a tree in a pot inside the living room that ate flies. I became very fond of that pot plant and tried hard to catch its dinner for it every day, taking flies home in a little glass jar from the office. Birdlife was profuse at CRB and I took great pleasure in seeing wildlife again. The air was fresh up on our hill and the view from the Mini Court, if you didn't look down into the crater, was magnificent. Across the river that separated us from the mainland were green and brown paddy fields, a charming village, very rural, and, rising from the paddies further out, were majestic mountain ranges, which were swathed in mist in the early morning.

A feeling of peace, of winding down, of relief, came over me the first evening as I sat on the trailer steps sipping a drink, waiting for the PX commander who had met my flight to call for me to take me to the mess for dinner.

I came down to earth the next day when I was shown where I would work. It was in a quonset hut, a metal semicircular tunnel-like structure that had no airconditioning and no glass in the windows. Each afternoon, the winds whipped up the sand and it blew through the openings in the walls and stung me. The office was overcrowded and stifling inside.

My workmates, with the exception of the American in charge of the Personnel Office, were entirely Vietnamese. In the adjoining end of the hut was the Accounts Branch, and in there was another Australian, a male accountant, and several Filipino men with whom I made friends.

I don't think any of the Vietnamese staff, who were all country folk, had ever seen a white girl up close before. When I was introduced to them, they felt the hairs on my forearms, exclaiming over them. They fingered my hair and dress too. They seemed to be pleased with me.

The office had a *mamasan*, an old lady with only one tooth left in her head like a front fang. She swept the office, dusted the desks and fixed the Viet staff's lunches. The Viets were not allowed to eat in the messes and brought lunch pails to work with them each day. They were transported on and off the base in disgusting cattle cars, large wooden trailers with no windows or air, and with armed GI guards on them. You would have thought they were the enemy, the way they were treated.

Mamasan loved me and fussed around me all day long, dusting my desk as I was trying to work, touching my hair and neck. She brought me French bread from the village and little gifts. One day she brought me an egg, but it was a funny, soft-skinned, black egg. I looked at it and wrinkled by nose. *Mamasan* squeaked, 'Ooh, ooh,' telling me with her hands that I should taste it first. Mel, one of the Filipinos from the accounts office, came in and said, surprised, 'Why, that's *baloot*.' The Viets called it a 'thousand-day-old egg', and it was made by taking a fertilised egg from under a hen when the chick was about half-developed inside, then burying the egg for 'a thousand days' or, in reality, about two months. The shell would soften and the inside become black. I couldn't bring myself to eat it, but Mel relieved me of my egg and bit into it happily. He crunched the bones and beak and picked tiny feathers from his teeth. It was certainly not my idea of a delicacy.

My job was interesting. I had to recruit and place Vietnamese into the jobs available at the PX stores and offices at CRB and other major Second Corps centres. In the training centre, Viet girls were given a good grounding in store and inventory management, accounting machine and cash register operation, food outlet management, typing and rudimentary office work. Vietnamese were hired and given on-the-job training in electronics and airconditioning mechanics, as truck drivers, forklift operators and warehousemen, as well as the office jobs. Because every Vietnamese man with any fighting ability was in the armed forces, the men who came to work for the PX system were either old or disabled. Throughout the country, I had seen women doing the jobs that men would have done in normal circumstances — digging ditches, climbing rickety bamboo scaffolding with loads of bricks, driving trucks, labouring on big engineering works. The Vietnamese women carried the country on their backs during the war. They kept their families together, fed and clothed them, while their menfolk were in the armed forces, and they moved the country ahead by sheer physical hard work. The women of Vietnam were truly the backbone of the country.

During my second month at CRB, the PX announced it was cutting our overtime. Most of the money I had saved since coming to the country was in overtime pay and now that the regular work hours were deemed to be 48, with no overtime, I had less pay and more leisure time in which to figure out ways of supplementing my dwindling salary. Somehow the Americans figured that a Filipino's regular work week was 40 hours, so the Filipinos still received eight hours of overtime pay a week. The result was that the poor bloody Aussie worker was on the lowest salary in the country. The Yanks sure had a funny idea of equality.

I took up running cases of Coke to the Australian air base at Phan Rang and bringing back Aussie beer to sell to the Yanks. Slouch hats I could sell to the Yanks for $200 each, a profit to me of $198 on each one. At the checkpoint over the river, I never had any trouble with the guards searching my jeep or PX vehicle. All I had to do was smile at them. The 50-mile drive south-west to Phan Rang was dangerous though, so I always took along a gunner. One young chap sat next to me in the vehicle, his M16 at the ready, until I noticed that he had the clip in back to front. I had to give him a lesson on loading his rifle. Poor little soldier.

The first time I visited the Aussie air base, the fellows were extremely surprised to see me walk in. I was made to feel at home, offered a can of beer and one man took me to the store where I purchased food items I had not seen for more than 15 months — Big Sister mushrooms in butter sauce, jars of Vegemite, the yeast extract that Australians love and everyone else in the world hates, Minties, Aussie cigarettes. I also bought a beach towel with the RAAF badge on it to use on the beach at Cam Ranh.

The base had a dog called Asco, just a mutt but a loveable, faithful animal. Whenever the alert siren went, Asco would always be first to the bunker. He would give a great howl, then run flat out. Whenever the base had practise alerts they would announce over the speakers, 'This is a practise only, ignore the siren.' Of course, Asco didn't know that. He would start running and, halfway to the bunker, stop, look around and realise he was the only one running. He would flatten his ears and give a shit-eating grin, and slink away in self-imposed disgrace. The RAAF boys ran a practise alert just so I could see Asco run.

During April, General Eisenhower died and the military observed three days of official mourning. Chapel services were held twice a day and I was surprised by the sincere grief shown by the American servicemen. Australians never got carried away by the death of any general or politician the way Americans did.

In the Personnel Office one mail call, my boss opened up a little box from home. In it was a soggy marshmallow and chocolate egg. 'Say, Holly, it's Easter,' he cried. We had forgotten about Easter. It was then we realised that we had become so involved with our Viet staff, their problems, customs and holidays that the outside world had faded from us. It just didn't seem real any more.

True to my promise to the girls in Saigon, I put out feelers to see where we might organise regular get-togethers. The CPOs at the naval base had parties, but not the officers, and the chiefs said they were not set up to have females in, so that wiped that out. The army base was a complete write-off. It was full of racial discontent between the white and black enlisted men; the MPs in jeeps with spotlights patrolled the camp nightly, and squads with fire hoses and tear gas moved between the barracks, ready for the first sign of fighting between the men. Although the barracks and main base were about 3km from the Mini Court, every so often at night I could hear shots. Twelve armed guards were placed around the Mini Court to protect us. I heard that a US senator was on his way to Cam Ranh to hear claims of racial discrimination. I made up my mind that it was time someone spoke out for the Aussies, who were definitely suffering racial discrimination in their salaries, mess hall, postal privileges, and, not least, PX privileges.

At the army mess hall, I had noticed that Filipinos hung back at meal times until all the Americans had been fed, entering only when there was no queue left. I asked Mel why.

'We have been told that we are Third Country Nationals and must wait until all the Americans have eaten before entering the mess hall,' he told me.

'But you're direct-hire employees,' I told him. 'If the regulations are being observed properly, you are entitled to eat *before* the Red Cross girls, and before the fat-cat civilians who work for Pacific Architects and Engineers, and for RMK-BRJ.'

I strode up to the sergeant on the door of the mess hall and told him that we were eating *now*. I pushed Mel ahead of me.

'*You* can come in now,' the sergeant said, 'but that lot had better wait till we're all finished up in here first.'

'Up yours,' I told him, pushing Mel through the door. The other Filipino men followed us in. An officer strode through the room and ordered the Filipinos out.

'You remove the Red Cross girls and the Yank civilians who are not direct-hire employees and then we'll go,' I said to him.

I quoted regulations at him, learned from my job in personnel. We were certainly entitled to eat with the Americans and it was ridiculous to expect us to eat scraps. The officer repeated what the sergeant had said — that I could eat now, but the others must wait.

'Why me?' I snarled. 'Is it because I look like you, with white skin and round eyes?'

We stood our ground and ate there and then. Every lunch hour for a week, I accompanied the Filipinos from the office to the mess hall and we stood in line and were served as we came. But when I ate elsewhere, the damn Filipinos moved to the end of the line again. They encouraged discrimination.

The air base had its racial problems, too. An air force major told me that there was one extraordinary incidence of prejudice — every night for a week two white airmen had been beheaded, their bodies left in the streets. One night one poor fellow lived to tell that he had been chopped at by axe-wielding black men, whose name tags had been removed from their uniforms. An all-out search ensued, and all black airmen were lined up for examination. As the major passed down the line, every single one of them had removed their name tags. So much for the 'brotherhood' of man. The murderers were never caught, but the killings stopped.

Kerry had rung to tell me that commissary privileges in Saigon had been withdrawn from the military, because Korean, Filipino and Thai troops had consistently cleaned out the store to resell the food on the black market. She said that at last she could buy hairspray and Tampax in the PX too before the Koreans heard about it, because she had asked Colonel Newman to tell the girls when a shipment was expected so they could get first bite at the apple. I remembered once on a trip to Vung Tau that the return flight was jam-packed with Korean troops. I was sitting with a colonel, who laughingly referred to the flights as 'the early morning garlic flight'. In answer to my question as to why so many Korean soldiers were on the plane, he said, 'There must be a shipment of cameras or something due in at the Cholon PX.' Sure enough, when I got back to head office, I checked. Five hundred cameras lasted one hour before the Koreans made off with the lot. I wondered who on the PX staff was leaking this information, and for how much?

Kerry invited me down to Saigon for a weekend to go out on a cruiser on the river with the Saigon Civil Affairs team. There was to be lunch and drinks on board, so I arranged a flight down and met the girls on Sunday for the day on the river. A staff of Viets on board lit our cigarettes, cooked and served lunch and kept our glasses full. We sat around in bikinis and shouted to the navy fellows on the big ships who hung over the side and whistled at us. I took a swim in the river, the Song Saigon, and wondered for weeks after if I would get hepatitis, as the water was filthy.

In the evening, we all went back to a house near Tan San Nhut where the girls had lined up dinner with the U-21 pilots. The U-21 was a little Lear jet, an eight-seater, for the exclusive use of generals, full colonels and civilians (Yank, of course) over the grade of 13. And the girls.

I reported that I had been made welcome at the 12th Tactical Fighter Wing, comprising three squadrons of F-4 Phantom jet pilots. One squadron, the 559th, or Billygoats, had offered to organise a party the next Saturday night to meet the Saigon ladies. All the girls said they would come and immediately asked the U-21 boys to fly them up. They said they would. Gail looked thoughtful.

'So, you think the Billygoats would mind if I asked Don to meet me there?' she asked. 'It's halfway between Saigon and Da Nang and an ideal opportunity for us to meet again.'

I said, 'Who cares?' and Gail decided she would ring Don to organise it.

When I got back to Cam Ranh, the Billygoats had decided that I should be made an honorary Billygoat and they measured me up for a party suit — a proper flight suit in bright blue with my name, wings, Billygoat patch and American flag on it. This is what the guys wore to mess parties and I was thrilled to be getting one. They promised to send my measurements off to Bangkok and to have it made in time for the party. I stood on a chair in the bar while they measured me, amid much laughter (and embarrassment on my part), then they went into a huddle to decide what my 'rank' on the suit should be. I couldn't wait for it to be made.

The Billygoats decided that the party should be an outdoor barbecue as there was still time before the monsoon season to have open-air functions. As Cam Ranh had only had rocket attacks three times in the previous year, I was looking forward to a party that, for once, would be uninterrupted by a Red Alert.

Chapter Eleven

BILLYGOATS, HAMMERS AND SHARKBAITS

THE GIRLS ARRIVED on Saturday evening, with their long dresses on hangers ready for the evening's festivities. They were shown to quarters to change and I drove over from the Mini Court to the air base to collect Gail. Don had arrived earlier and was waiting at my trailer for her. We ate a snack together and I didn't lay eyes on either one of them again until Sunday night when Don left and I drove Gail to the airport to meet up with the other girls. She couldn't wipe the smile off her face. When I waved goodbye to Don from the army airstrip, he hopped into the plane, took off, then circled overhead doing some trick acrobatics (loop-the-loop) for me. I suppose it was the same as tooting the horn to say goodbye when leaving by car.

My party suit had arrived. I thought I looked beautiful in it. Some of the air force nurses had party suits and mine was exactly the same, except for two things — my wings had

a little red heart in the centre and the rank on my shoulders
was the medical symbol for female. Later that evening, when
I was dancing with a two-star general, he examined my
shoulders and was puzzled by my 'rank'.

'Female, Sir,' I told him.

He took a step backwards, stood gravely to attention,
and saluted. 'I salute a higher rank,' he said.

The party was well under way in the Billygoat club.
Outside on the patio was a huge barbecue, behind which a
wooden cut-out of a billygoat was hanging on the wall.
Lighting from behind the cut-out illuminated it in
silhouette. It had two little red lights for testicles, which
flashed on and off.

Dinner was a whole roast pig and the squadron doctor
carved with much show and saying 'Scalpel please'. We sat at
long trestle tables to eat, meeting and mixing with the nicest
bunch of guys any of us had yet met in Vietnam. They were
all good-looking, daring, dashing and exciting. I could see
the Saigon crowd were really enjoying themselves.

Inside the club was a bar, which stretched the width of
the room at one end. A game was started up called 'Carrier
Landings'. A pilot had to pick his wing man (usually a girl)
and then climb up onto the bar. Zippo lighters, lit, were
placed down the room to form a runway, then the floor was
hosed down to make it slippery. The object was to do a
bellyflop off the bar, hanging onto the pilot, and slide along
the water down the runway, just like landing on an aircraft
carrier. Three fellows broke their ribs, I got a cut eye and

several other girls were damaged. We all went over to the hospital to get stitched up.

Too drunk to feel any pain, I danced the night away until the party was raided by the two other squadrons — Hammers in red party suits and Sharkbaits in green. Someone from the Billygoats had been caught erasing the sixth and seventh letters of the word Sharkbaits outside their club, replacing them with the letters 'S' and 'H'. So, in retaliation they, the Sharkshits and Hammers, raided the Billygoat party. Fire hoses were brought out to repel the attack and fellows were falling over tables and girls, wrestling and punching at each other.

We slept over at the 559th in various places. I couldn't get anyone to drive me home. Jeff had come to the party and was so drunk he was walking around with a broken thong flapping around his leg, shouting, 'My mate Holly will drive me home. No one but my mate Holly can TOUCH my jeep!' His mate Holly was incapable of driving any jeep, so I herded Jeff into an empty room with double bunks and we climbed in, me in the top bunk. During the night, a very drunk and irate pilot tipped Jeff out of the bunk onto the floor, climbed over Jeff's prone body and into his own bed. Jeff never moved till reveille.

We spent the next day at the air force beach. The long coastline had been divided up into air force, army and navy beaches, and no one trespassed. The air force beach was by far the best set up. In fact, everything air force was better than navy or army. On the beach was a permanent bar, barbecue facilities, a covered dance floor and a lifeguard's chair and reel. I noticed several of the fellows wriggling on their stomachs as they sunbaked, looks of absolute pain on their faces. They had had vasectomies, compliments of Uncle Sam. This operation was still a hassle to get in the States and so many wives had written to say they were enjoying a year off the Pill that the fellows had had the operation done at the hospital at Cam Ranh.

We jogged up and down the beach. One of the girls had brought a boomerang with her and we all practised throwing it. We surfed and swam until it was too hot to be out in the sun, then gathered on the dance floor for food and drink. I felt I was going to love being posted to Cam Ranh Bay.

After May Day, enemy activity heated up. The JP4 fuel line containing jet fuel was sabotaged and burned fiercely for hours. We started to get rockets lobbed on us from the mountains across the river at regular intervals, but all they ever seemed to hit were the toilets. It became a standard joke on the army base to wave a white flag at the mountains before entering the toilet block. Little Miss Quynh, one of my favourite staff members, was raped by two black Americans and badly bashed about the face. The next day, I was bailed up on the boardwalk by a group of black soldiers, who spat at me and sneered about the White Australia Policy. MPs came running and broke up the mob, but I was left trembling and scared. I was so glad Australia didn't have the racial problems America obviously had.

The problem got worse day by day. It was a growing thing that you could almost see and hear. One of the Viet girls who worked in the pizza hut and who was four months' pregnant was knocked down by a black man, who stomped on her face. She sustained a broken jaw and nose and went into shock within minutes. She lost her baby. The white enlisted men were not much better. They wore peace symbols on their uniforms and beads and flowers. The officers didn't have the guts to stop them. It would have meant a punch in the face. I was becoming more frightened of the army man than of the Vietcong!

I was sleeping over at the air base one night when Cong sappers made a daring raid by paddling across the river and running through the Convalescent Centre, throwing satchel charges onto the beds of wounded men. Sirens sounded and the base burst into full Red Alert. I climbed under the bed, shivering with fear in the dark. I heard the wire screen on the window above my bed rip and something was thrown on the floor just a few feet from my head. I could see little red dots in the dark and I watched them disappear one by one. When the All Clear sounded, I crawled out from under the bed and switched on the light. Four sticks of dynamite taped together lay on the floor; the wicks had somehow gone out. I sank to my knees, just staring at the sticks for what seemed like an eternity.

Just a week later, the air base was hit by more rockets, which damaged buildings and killed several men. But this time it was not the Vietcong, but Korean troops with bad aim. They were stationed just west of the mountains and had been trying to lob shells over the crest onto the eastern side of the mountains. There were apologies all round when the mistake was discovered.

By this time I had found myself a lover, a dashing Phantom pilot. His name was Garry and we met and made love in the oddest places. There was a water tower right in the middle of the air base with a tarpaulin cover tied over it. Garry and I would climb the long ladder up and slither over the side, rolling down to the centre of the tarpaulin. Giggling and trying not to shake the tower, we would undress each other and make love, lying back afterwards to watch the night sky light up with rockets and flares. The only time we made love on the water tower during the day, a chopper flew over and hovered, the guys yelling encouragement to us. The news was all over the base within minutes of the chopper landing.

Garry got hold of the maps of where the mines were laid on the beaches and we carefully tiptoed through the minefield to a secret spot near the lapping water where we could swim naked and lie together on the beach. It was terrific to play in the surf then crawl exhausted onto the sand and make love. But the chopper pilots found us again, so we had to give that spot up too.

One working day, Garry rang me from the air base to tell me to quit work for the afternoon and meet him at Teeny Weeny Airport, the army airstrip just near my office. I told my boss I was off to visit a couple of PX stores to check on the trainees and raced down to the airstrip. The chopper pilots were all sitting around with their feet on desks and when I came puffing in, they all grinned.

'At it again, Holly?' they asked.

I said with dignity, 'I'm being picked up here to go visit some stores.'

'A likely story,' said one, but they accepted it and talked to me of other things until Garry landed in a small four-seater 0-2 plane. This aircraft was used in conjunction with the Phantoms. It was a spotter plane, the pilot going out first in this little plane to seek enemy movement, reporting back by radio to the air base to scramble the jets, who flew to the location with their bombs. The 0-2 pilot would then dive in low, firing Willy Pete (white phosphorous) rockets into the enemy area, telling the Phantom pilots to 'Hit my smoke' or 'Hit 50 metres above my smoke', thus giving direction to the fast-moving Phantoms so they could drop their bombs with accuracy. After the Phantoms had done their job and gone back to base, the 0-2 pilot would come in close to the area and examine the results of the bombing and make a report back to base by radio.

Garry, of course, should not have been flying the 0-2. He had borrowed it from a friend in another squadron. It was a funny little plane; its civilian name was the Cessna Super Skymaster.

I climbed aboard and we took off, heading north-west over VC country. It was terribly hot, so we climbed up to about 10,000 feet and wound down the windows for coolness. I felt so good with the cold breeze blowing around my body that I slipped off my cotton shirt. Garry, in the left seat, eyed me with a look I had come to know well.

'Not up here?' I asked, hoping I had read his look correctly.

'Why not?'

He slipped out of his flight suit, holding the steering apparatus with his knees as he shrugged off the top half, then I pushed down his zipper and dragged off his boots. Both naked, I climbed onto his lap, facing him, smothering him with kisses as he tried to keep the plane steady. It was the most satisfying, deliriously joyful and probably quickest screw I have ever had. We lost only 3,000 feet in altitude in the climax.

Puffing and panting, grinning at each other, we sat back naked in our seats while Garry sorted out the position of the plane. Voices were shouting at us through the earphones of his helmet, 'Come in ... come in ... location?' He winked at me. 'I'm supposed to be working, looking for Cong activity.' He replaced his helmet and was all business for a minute, reporting back to base.

I looked up. Damn it all, there were the chopper pilots again, waving at us. I hoped they hadn't seen us. We just couldn't seem to escape their prying eyes.

Garry decided to give me a lesson in flying the plane. He feathered the back engine and showed me how to 'kick start' it again. Then he feathered the front engine and the bloody thing wouldn't kick over. Beads of sweat were rolling down his face and he looked worried. I wasn't worried. I had no idea of the danger we were in. I was still on cloud nine.

'We'll have to crash land,' he told me.

Fear gripped, my stomach turned over.

'What's wrong, the engine's still going, why can't we fly home?' I babbled.

Garry explained patiently to me that we had enough fuel to the back engine only to get us to a deserted airstrip he knew of just north of our position. It was most probably in enemy hands or at least the enemy would be close by in the jungle. We needed both engines and both fuel tanks to get us back to Cam Ranh Bay. He told me we had a choice. We could make it to the deserted airstrip and he would give his location to CRB air base, which would dispatch an aircraft immediately to pick us up. That could take more than an hour and, in the meantime, we could be captured. My fate at the hands of North Vietnamese or Vietcong was certain. I shuddered.

'What's the alternative?' I asked.

'We can climb on one engine to about 15,000 feet, then I will feather the remaining engine and let us drop. As we dive, I can try to simultaneously start both engines. If they both start, we're home and hosed,' he told me.

'And if they don't?'

'And if they don't, my girl,' he leaned over and held me close, 'they find our bodies together in the wreck.'

I thought about it for a while. Garry had left the decision entirely up to me.

'Let's give the kick-start dive a go.' Once the decision was made, we both felt better, but as we climbed slowly into the sky, I looked at the sun and then the green trees below and wondered if it would be the last thing I ever saw. I stared at Garry, trying to imprint his face on my mind as if this would carry through with me if we died.

'This is it!' he said, and leant over and kissed me.

'Where the hell are our chopper friends now that we really need them?'

I held the seat tightly. Garry switched off both engines and we took a dive, plummeting so fast towards the earth that I nearly passed out. When it seemed as if we would certainly splatter the jungle, Garry frantically pressed switches and buttons, working furiously.

A miracle happened. Both engines kicked over and we shuddered then swung into an upward swoop, both shouting and cheering. We hugged and kissed, crying with relief.

Back at Teeny Weeny Airport when Garry dropped me off before returning to the air base, he hopped out of the plane and examined it. Bits of green foliage were caught in the fuselage and in the corners of the wing struts. It had been a close shave.

A week later, when I was at the air base, Garry took me to the flight lines and showed me the little 0-2. On its nose had been stencilled HOLLY in memory of our epic flight. I had certainly earned my wings that day.

I could now claim to be the only female to have joined the Mile High Club in the Vietnam War.

Chapter Twelve

OFF WE GO INTO THE WILD BLUE YONDER

'BULLSHIT.' 'BULLSHIT AND bullshit again!'

I stormed around the office, flapping the letter I had been handed. I had never read so much crap in my entire life.

'As a result of a recent wage study in Australia …' I read out loud to the Vietnamese sitting around all nodding sagely at me, uncomprehending. 'Whose leg are they trying to pull? This wage increase is a direct result of my complaint to the Senator from California!'

It certainly was good to get a 60 per cent wage increase, but it brought the Australians' salaries only up to the level of other Third Country Nationals. It had absolutely nothing to do with comparable jobs in Australia — and the bullshit about 'locally hired Australian citizen employees' was just Yank crap, too. There was no such animal. *Every* Australian in-country had been hired in Sydney and brought to Vietnam to work for the PX on a contract that had been twisted and broken by the PX chiefs without a glimmer of conscience. Now, after I had stood in line with a group of black Americans, and had taken my turn in the tent to tell of my personal racial discrimination experiences, the PX was glossing over the whole thing and trying to make it look as though the wage increase was a result of their own generosity.

The Senator had been surprised to see me. As the line shuffled closer to the tent flap, I had been able to hear raised and black voices saying, 'Now hear, man ...' and cool, calm replies from the Senator: 'I'm here to listen, tell me about it ...'

I had walked into the tent and introduced myself to the Senator when my turn came. I launched straight into the list of problems confronted by the Australian civilians, emphasising that we were direct-hire employees of the US Department of Defence in name only, and that we were denied mess hall privileges, postal and banking facilities, our purchasing power was limited to goods under $20 in the PX, our living allowance to live 'on the economy' was one-third of the US civilian's allowance to live on the same economy, and our biggest gripe of all — we were grossly underpaid for doing exactly the same jobs as the American civilians working for the same organisation. The Senator listened without interruption. I gave him a file I had prepared, listing all I had said and elaborating on it, with supporting facts and figures. He accepted it and said, 'This is really interesting. I have listened for two days to complaints of racial discrimination, but you are the first person to put facts on paper before me. I will certainly do something about it!' I left the tent hoping his words were not like so many other American words — pie in the sky.

I looked again at the letter in my hand and suddenly the humour of it all reached me. I had got what *I* wanted from the Yanks — and they had given it without losing 'face'. 'OK,' I thought, 'Now we'll call it quits.'

The commander of the area exchange called me and the Filipinos into his office a few days later and informed us that we were to be given postal privileges, but, he added, 'Only because you are all so isolated up here and there are no local post offices you can use.'

'About bloody time,' I thought, and added aloud, 'Thank you, Sir.'

Little did he know that we had all been using the APO system for months — ever since I arrived at Cam Ranh Bay and discovered that the Filipinos were unable to write home. I had made up a name and serial number and endorsed my letters home with that name, and received letters under that name, attending mail call quite openly to collect my letters. The Filipinos all used the one name, 'Sergeant C. Cordova'. It was a nice enough name for a Spanish-American and there were enough Latinos in the US Army for the name to go unnoticed. No one even noticed that every letter Sergeant C. Cordova sent went to the Philippines, just as all of Spec. 4 Rookwood's mail went to Sydney, Australia.

I had been spending more and more time at the air base, but Garry was due to go home soon and I was hoping somehow he could bequeath his jeep to me, as once he had gone I had no transport. I mentioned this to him and also to the Wing

Commander, who said he would try to do something about it.

A few nights later I was at the Billygoats' bar, happily getting sloshed, when the Wing Commander, Colonel Garcia, walked in and yelled, 'Hey Holly, come outside. I have a surprise for you.'

I got up and followed him, and the grinning Billygoats all followed us. Outside, on the roadway, was a massive machine with a great gun poking out the front of it. I stared in fascination.

'What is it?' I asked.

'Allow me to introduce you to your new vehicle,' the Wing Commander bowed, trying to hide his grin. 'It's an armoured personnel carrier and it's all yours, with my compliments.'

I looked up at the towering mass of metal, overawed by its size.

'Do I need a licence to drive it?' I inquired.

'No, but you'll need a few lessons,' Colonel Garcia replied, 'and I think we'd all better have a few more drinks before we start on the first lesson. As a matter of fact,' his grin broadened, 'your first lesson in driving an APC is — never try to climb into the thing if you're sober.'

So we went back into the bar and had several more drinks, until Colonel Garcia felt ripe enough to give me my first lesson. Then we all climbed aboard. I was pushed down a hole in the roof and my feet just touched the floor. Colonel Garcia donned rakish goggles, upside down, and climbed down behind me into the hole. It was a tight squeeze and he reached around me, placing my hands under his on the two sticks that came up out of the floor in front of us.

'These are what steer the thing,' he told me. 'If they are level, you go in a straight line. If you push one forward the track on that side pulls faster than the other track and you can turn corners.'

It sounded simple.

'OK then. Let's have a practice,' the Colonel said. 'Start her up, boys', and the engine purred into life.

He guided my hands on the sticks and we trundled heavily along the roadway between the clubs and hootches. I stood on tiptoe and could just see where we were going.

'We've got to get some speed up, get somewhere where we can give it a good run,' Colonel Garcia muttered and headed the APC out to the edge of the vast runway where the planes were lining up to take off. We stopped at the entrance to the runway. I could see the airport terminal a mile away across the other side of the massive runways and the lights of the control tower near it. Colonel Garcia pulled a walkie-talkie out of his pocket, pulled up the aerial and called the control tower. He spoke swiftly and quietly, in terminology I could not understand.

'OK now, all clear,' he said, and swung the APC out onto the runway, revving it up to full speed and showing me, with great delight, how to manoeuvre the machine.

'Where are all the planes?' I asked, frightened that we would be run down by a landing jet at any moment.

'No sweat, lady,' he told me. 'I have ordered the tower to keep them up in the air circling for 15 minutes, and to delay take-off for the ones on the ground. The airstrip is all ours for the next quarter-hour.'

What fun we had, tearing all around the Cam Ranh Bay air strips, in and out of hangers, up and down the runways, laughing and screaming. Some of the Billygoats had perched themselves on top of the APC and a couple were down inside the machine doing things with the engine, I thought. The doctor was brought along in case of casualties. We were all roaring drunk, they with booze, me with power. It was exhilarating.

At the end of 15 minutes, we headed off the runways and into the terminal building to buy ice-cream from the PX vendor just inside the door. I parked the APC right outside the door and the boys lifted me down. We all ran inside the terminal, still laughing, to buy our cones.

A C-141 had landed only about half an hour before our great excursion across the airfield and raw recruits with brand new shiny boots and uniforms, looking unaccustomed to holding rifles, were sitting in little groups inside the terminal. They all stared in wonder when a bunch of drunken, noisy pilots climbed out of the APC, but their mouths fell open when a miniskirted lady hopped out of the driver's hole closely followed by a full colonel.

'Welcome to Vietnam,' shouted Colonel Garcia, and he treated ice-creams all round to the open-mouthed soldiers.

We couldn't go back the way we had come, so we had to take the APC to the entrance of the terminal and back around the road that wound by the water to the bridge. At the bridge, when we should have turned left to go around the end of the runway and back to the air base, Colonel Garcia decided we should take the APC for a run down to the army base to see the top-ranking military man on the island, General Seagrove. So we roared off down the road at full speed, in the dark and with no lights, gun muzzle swinging to the time of the Billygoats singing. I learnt a few rude songs that night, as well as how to drive an APC.

As we rounded a bend in the road, with the water on our right and the hills leading up to the mortuary on our left, I could have sworn I saw jeep lights bumping up the grassy slope towards the swamp that separated the mortuary from the road. But they were gone in a flash so I assumed I must have been seeing things.

We came to General Seagrove's large tent and I was going to park at the foot of the little hill it was on, when Colonel Garcia told me that an APC could go anywhere, so I pushed it up the hill, intent on parking right at the General's door. There was a terrible zinging sound of tearing wires and someone on top of the APC said 'Christ!' I stopped the machine and we climbed out to see what had happened.

I had driven through the telecommunication wires that were the General's line to General Joseph's headquarters in Saigon, and his hotline to the States.

'Ouch,' said Colonial Garcia, and he looked around quickly. No one had come out of the tent to investigate, so we all quietly and quickly climbed back aboard the APC, reversed off the wires and hightailed it back to the air base. Colonel Garcia drove me home to the army base later that night in his jeep.

As we entered my trailer in the Mini Court, my roommate, Anna Campbell, the Special Services librarian, indicated to General Seagrove, who was sitting having a drink in our living room. He and Colonel Garcia were old buddies and the General said, 'Mel, you have no idea what happened to me tonight. I was driving over to the air base to see you and I was literally run off the road by a pack of louts in an APC.'

'Oh?' said the Colonel, clearing his throat. 'Did you see who it was?'

'No, damn it, too dark,' said the General, 'but I think they were some of your boys, Mel. They were singing "Off we go into the wild blue yonder" as they went past me. You had better find out who they were and let me know.'

'I promise I will try,' replied Colonel Garcia and winked at me. I knew then I could never take my APC over to the army base.

'Oh well,' I thought, 'I'll have to get a vehicle some other way.'

It took two days for the communication wires to be fixed and the General stormed around the base, angrily questioning men, seeking any clue as to how his wires had been brought down. I thanked my lucky stars it had not been raining that night, as no one had mentioned finding any APC tracks in the grassy hill leading up to the General's tent.

The day before Garry was due to leave Vietnam, he came to collect me early on Sunday morning in his jeep. Over his arm he carried a flight suit, with a major's rank on it. I was intrigued, as he wouldn't tell me what it was for.

'Just put it on,' he said, 'and come with me. I have a great surprise for you.'

We drove to the air base, but instead of heading to the Billygoats' area, he swung the jeep into the mass of buildings lining the airstrip.

'Wait here,' he ordered. 'I'll see if the coast is clear.'

I waited, mystified, until he came out of the door and beckoned me, putting a finger to his lips.

We hurried down a corridor, past closed doors, and he hustled me into a room. There were a couple of fellows waiting for us and they grabbed me and started pushing my legs into a funny rubber suit.

'Hey, hey,' I protested. 'What's going on?'

'You're coming on a mission with me, that's what,' said Garry. 'I'm leaving this place in style and my last flight is going to be a dilly!'

I nearly fainted with excitement. 'Do you mean you are actually taking me up in a Phantom jet?' I squeaked.

'Yup,' he said, and pinched my bottom.

The two fellows were busily dressing me in the G-suit, or gravitational suit. They explained that it was full of little rubber bladders that would automatically fill up with air from a connection in the plane and would push the blood to my head, preventing me from blacking out when we 'pulled Gs'. They strapped a parachute to my back and through my legs, giving me rudimentary instructions on how to open it if we had to ditch. I hung onto every word, trying to memorise the procedure. My legs were trembling.

Then they sat me in a pilot's chair that was in the centre of the room, showing me the red handle between my knees, issuing the warning, 'Don't on any account touch that handle. It is an ejection handle.'

'In fact,' added Garry, 'don't touch a *thing* once you are inside the plane. You could send us off into eternity.'

They explained about the 'hot mike' and the 'cold mike'. The hot mike was when Garry was talking to ground control and, as I would not be able to tell whether the mike was hot or cold (connected to me only), I was not to speak unless Garry said my name. If ground control heard a female voice from the jet, we would all be court-martialled and probably shot! Or so Garry said.

Someone popped his head around the door and said, 'All clear', so we shuffled down the corridor, bypassing the usual scramble room, out a side door and onto the runway. Two F-4s were parked there, ready for flight. My stomach was turning over, with fear and terrible excitement.

Garry stuck a helmet on my head and tucked my hair up under it. He pulled the visor down over my eyes. 'Just walk casually out to the plane and around to the starboard side,' he told me. I did as I was told. Several other fellows nonchalantly followed me out, and they hoisted me up into the back cockpit of the plane. One ran around to the port side and climbed a ladder, leaning into the plane to connect my G-suit to a hose outlet. 'Sit tight and good luck,' he whispered, tapping me on the helmet a couple of times. He disappeared down the ladder.

Garry climbed up into the front cockpit and busied himself with his check list. He didn't turn around or even acknowledge my presence. I sat still, afraid to turn my head and look back at the scramble room. Two other fellows came out and climbed into the other jet and they, too, busied themselves with their heads down. We seemed to sit there for an eternity under the hot sun.

Garry started the engines and I heard him say through the earphones of my helmet that we were carrying five tonnes of bombs and our destination was Steel Tiger. My heart leapt. Steel Tiger, or ST, as it was listed on the flight lists pinned in the wing orderly room, was the code name used for flights over Hanoi. I felt faint again. A bloody bombing run over North Vietnam was bad enough, but my first ride in a Phantom, absolutely no knowledge of how to use a parachute, the chance of being ejected by mistake or even on purpose ... I counted all the black marks against this joy-ride and decided I wanted out. But we were now at the end of the runway, the cables had been attached to the plane to catapult us away and the engines were roaring as if they would take off on their own. I was stuck, like it or not.

I looked through the perspex shield, past the high back of Garry's seat and saw the other Phantom take off. Just then Garry gave a thumbs-up sign and I thought no more, as my body was wrenched backwards with such force I thought I would go through my seat.

Whoosh. My lungs were going to burst. I saw stars and we were off. We seemed to touch the runway only fleetingly before pulling into a back-breaking rise towards the sun. Within seconds, my body adjusted and I blinked and swallowed. My mouth was dry.

My earphones crackled. 'Holly, are you all right?' Garry's familiar voice sounded wonderful. I pressed the button on my mouthpiece and answered, 'I feel terrific.' It took a great effort to speak.

'Look down at Cam Ranh Bay,' said Garry.

'Where?' I asked, craning my neck.

He flipped the plane over, flying along upside down.

'There,' he said, 'just look up.'

'Oh!' What more could I say? Spread before me was the entire coastline, miniature and moving fast below us. A great feeling of complete joy welled up inside me. I wanted to sing. This was simply beautiful. Flying had never been like this before. I didn't want to come down again. I was in heaven.

We flipped back over and caught up with the other plane, then flew in formation, heading north. I was glad the cockpits were completely separate, because I was in such a high state of joy that if I had got my hands on Garry, we would have joined the Mile High Club again, there and then, at Mach 2.

Garry had warned me of what would happen when we broke the sound barrier, but I was hardly aware that we had. I didn't want to miss a single nuance of feeling, a single emotion, a single roll of the plane during that entire experience. But once we had settled into our flight pattern, high above the ground, it was really no different to any other flight. So I just sat still, listening to the exchanges between Garry and the ground, and the other pilots in our twin plane.

I recognised Da Nang when we flew high overhead and the country from there on became very mountainous and green. The coast was far away to our starboard and we moved inland heading north-west.

'Holly,' said Garry. 'We are over Laos now,' and I looked down at my one and only glimpse of Laos. It looked the same as South Vietnam from the air.

We swung around towards the east, the pilots intent on finding their mark. I heard them say they had reached target and they discussed their orders for dropping their loads.

'Holly, we are going down now,' said Garry, 'hold tight.'

We 'pulled Gs' in a tight arc, doubling back the way we had just flown but right down close to the ground. Now I could feel our speed and the thrill of flying hit me again like a sledgehammer. My heart raced as we swooped in low over the jungle and the plane seemed to dance a backward step as the bombs rocketed away from us. We made only one run, then climbed steeply away from the destruction below us. As we circled again overhead, I looked down to the smoking pile to try to see what the target had been. It looked like the rest of the jungle to me, but I supposed the enemy was down there somewhere.

The other plane dived down, dropping its bombs within metres of ours, then swooped back up to the skies to meet with us. The pilots exchanged talk, estimating their 'kill'.

'All bombs away at 11:15 hours,' I heard someone say.

'Now let's get to the rendezvous.'

We flew south-east. 'Holly, Hanoi is just over to your left,' Garry told me, but although I searched the horizon, I could not see the city.

We came out over the ocean and circled for a while. The pilots were searching the skies, looking for the 'rendezvous'. I saw a speck in the distance, which, when it came closer, was a large aircraft. It came so close to us I thought we would hit it and my hand crept towards the red handle between my legs.

'Holly, we are going to refuel from this plane' Garry told me. 'It's a KC-135 tanker or, in your language, a Boeing 707, and we are going to come up under its belly to refuel, so don't get a shock.'

We followed the tanker closely and I could see lights blinking on and off under its belly. The lights were telling

Garry his position and he jockeyed the plane as if he was putting a horse to a jump. A large, flying boom swung down from the tanker and it came right at me, sliding above my cockpit and into the plane behind me. Clang. We were connected. We were tied to the tanker like mating dragonflies. We circled, refuelling.

We cut free when the fuelling was completed and pulled back to allow the other plane its turn. I had my ever-present camera with me and madly snapped off shots of the tanker, the boom coming over my head, then the other plane during its refuelling process.

'Right,' I heard someone say as the other plane broke away from the tanker, 'home we go.'

'Holly, like to try some moon-rolling?' said Garry and, without waiting for a reply, he aimed the plane at the sun high overhead and put it into a slow roll, climbing as we rolled and using the sun as his guide. It was marvellous and I cheered him on. We flitted and played, flapping around the skies as if we owned them.

At last I could see Cam Ranh airstrip below, as we shot overhead for the final turn back to land. Garry was busy with his landing business and I just sat back, sorry that the flight was over and a little apprehensive about getting out of the jet and back into the building without being discovered. We came low over the end of the runway and I was unprepared for the absolute shock of the landing. I had forgotten that they used a hook and parachute to land the jets and, as we touched down and the hook below the plane grabbed the wire stretched across the runway, I belted forward in my seat, almost throwing up with fright. I thought we had crashed!

When the plane idled back along the side of the runway to the disembarkation area, I was puffing and exhausted. I pulled off my face mask and rubbed the tender areas around my nose and mouth. My breath was raw in my lungs. We pulled up outside the building and the canopy above my head flew open. The air was muggy and hot after the oxygen I had been breathing for the past few hours. I started to sweat under my helmet.

We stopped and some guys came running out to meet us. I kept my head averted, but there was no fooling them. One young airman let out a whoop. 'What have we here?' he cried. Garry shushed him urgently. 'Keep it to yourself,' he begged, and I climbed out shakily and moved as fast as I could to the scramble room. As I pushed open the door and tried to move inconspicuously inside, a bottle of champagne was waved under my nose and my helmet was pulled from my head. I looked around wildly, feeling naked. The entire wing seemed to be there, everyone waving filled glasses and shouting congratulations at me. Penny had been right when she had said it was impossible to keep a secret in this place. The whole world had turned out to welcome me home, it seemed. Garry was grabbed as he came through the door and his look of absolute fright turned to pink pleasure as he realised he was not in trouble with anyone for taking me up. He had really left his mark on the wing and his farewell party that afternoon, punctuated by the war as pilots came and went from missions in their planes outside, was a truly memorable occasion.

Garry left for home the next afternoon and I cried a little as I watched him walk up the steps onto the big Freedom Bird that would fly him home to the States. After gaining my wings in such a medley of fantastic ways, always with Garry as my cohort in crime, I knew I would miss him and probably die of boredom now that he was gone.

But I was wrong.

Chapter Thirteen

STEALING CAN BE FUN TOO!

FROM WHERE I was sitting in the back of the C-130 aircraft, I could see everybody. I had my back to the entrance to the cockpit and was hanging onto the webbing until take-off was completed, after which I would move up into the cockpit to talk to the crew and perhaps wangle a turn at flying the big machine. I had become extremely keen on learning to fly and every opportunity I found (and they were numerous), I took over the controls of the aircraft. I had flown 0-2s, 0-10s (both twin boom aircraft), I had had a short try on the Phantom but had given up in fright, a C-7A, a U-21 (from Saigon to Qui Nhon to collect a general), and had flown many times at the controls of C-130s, the big Hercules transport planes.

I had flown a group of soldiers from Saigon up to Cam Ranh Bay on a return trip from a party a month or so earlier and had sat in the right seat and done the radio work as well as the flying; but when I left the plane and walked across the tarmac, one of the soldiers from the plane caught up and fell into step with me. 'Have you collected your flight pay yet?' he whispered. 'I saw you flying that plane.' So I knew that I had to be careful not to get any of the flight crew court-martialled.

This lot of passengers looked as though they would not notice my disappearance into the cockpit. There were two travelling bands, one Filipino group who sat quietly, and a loud-mouthed cheaply dressed Australian group. I looked at them and resolved to hail from Boston if they asked me where I was from. I didn't want to be associated with *that* type. Their girl singers all looked like hussies and the guys looked stupid with their long hair. 'Give me a clean-cut Yank any day,' I thought.

Settled down the middle of the plane, on the red criss-crossed webbing straps, were several Vietnamese soldiers and their wives and families. Every time a Viet was posted to a different area by the ARVN, he could take along his family and his few belongings. Squawking in a coup were chickens and the family pig was on a leash, curled up asleep with one of the children.

A few American soldiers sat at the rear, lounging against the fuselage, cigarettes and Zippos ready for when the take off was completed and the word was given that they could smoke.

We had left Cam Ranh Bay air terminal more than an hour and a half before, but instead of heading straight for Saigon we had flown north to Nha Trang. I had asked the navigator why and he told me that we had to make a stopover to pick up a severely wounded man at Nha Trang who had no other transport to Saigon, and who was in urgent need of hospital treatment. At the time I thought this was stupid, as there was a fully equipped hospital at Cam Ranh Bay and a medivac flight to Clark Air Base in the Philippines was as quick as a flight to Saigon. 'Still,' I thought, looking at the solder lying on the stretcher at the end of the plane, with the nurse checking his drip every so often, 'the military moves in mysterious ways, and mine is not to question why.'

I felt the plane lift off the runway, heading out over the South China Sea and, at the same instant, I felt it lurch violently and slew to port. Then I heard the rocket hit. Funny how the noise carries after the motion. The port windows were ablaze with firelight coming from one of the engines and there was pandemonium in the plane as everyone rushed to that side to try to see what had happened.

I raced into the cockpit, where the pilot was calmly talking to ground control. He had cut the fuel to the damaged engine and the crew was busy assessing the damage as best they could. One of the crew made his way past me to the cockpit entrance and shouted to everyone to resume their seats and be calm. The poor Vietnamese didn't know what was happening. The little children were crying and their mothers hugged them close. I went to the Vietnamese families and said as best as I could in their language that they should sit still and be quiet, although in literal translation I told them, 'Sit down and shut up', but I made by voice as kindly as I could and then said 'Xin loi' (sorry about that) to try to explain my language deficiency. One of the mothers held my hand and nodded to me, smiling tremulously. I think she understood what I was trying to do to help them.

The Filipinos panicked, beating their hands on the fuselage and screaming, 'Let us out.' I shouted at them in my best Filipino, 'Katahimikan' (silence!), adding in rough Spanish, just in case they understood that better, 'Yo golpe', which I thought meant 'I'll bash you'. It was a threat I had heard my Filipino workmates using on each other and it worked with this lot. They turned and stared at me, then sat down quietly. Peace reigned.

One of the crew came back and stood on the ladder to the cockpit. 'May I have your attention, please,' he said, shouting above the noise of the engines.

'We have been hit and have lost a port engine, but ...,' he raised his hands to quiet the growl of consternation that arose, 'we can fly on three engines, so don't worry. We can't go back to Nha Trang because it is now under Red Alert and we can't land at Cam Ranh because we have to use up all our fuel before we attempt a landing. So we are going to fly slowly but surely to Saigon and make a crashlanding at Tan San Nhut. We will alert them of our condition before we land, so everything possible will be done to bring this bird down safely. All I can do is ask you all to sit tight and be still and quiet for the rest of the trip. I will talk to you again just prior to landing to give you emergency landing procedures. Thank you.'

He disappeared into the cockpit.

'Oh, I forgot,' his head popped out again. 'Definitely no smoking until we land.'

It was a long, tension-filled flight south towards Saigon. We flew high so as to be out of reach of enemy ground fire or rockets. Someone strummed a guitar and sang a quiet, sad song. The American soldiers played dice.

We circled Tan San Nhut Airport, in wide circles, for more than two hours. I looked through the window down at the bright lights of Saigon and wished fervently that I was safely on the ground. I was very frightened at the thought of the landing we had to make, every circle of the plane taking us nearer to it.

A crew member came out of the cockpit and clapped his hands for attention.

'We are about to commence our descent to the airport,' he announced. 'We will spiral downwards from the position almost directly above the landing zone, so that we don't attract ground fire from the airport perimeter. When we are just about to attempt our landing, I will give three blasts on this whistle,' he blew the whistle three times to show us,' and then you will take your landing positions.'

He moved down the ladder and stepped through the webbing to the centre of the aircraft, taking hold of a Viet soldier to demonstrate.

'Three blasts,' he blew the whistle again, 'and you will do *this*.'

He made the Viet kneel facing the cockpit, within a square of webbing ropes, then gently pressed his face to the floor, placing his hands at the cross ties above his head. He then grabbed a military sack, a long cylindrical bag and placed it between the Viet's head and the webbing that ran horizontally across the plane. He then stood behind the Viet and pushed his rump roughly, to show that his head bumped into the bags, which were held in place by the roping.

'You *bic?*' he asked the Vietnamese men and women.

'*Da!*' they all nodded.

'Does everybody understand?' he looked around. Everyone nodded. 'OK then, let's have a practice.'

I placed my Pan Am bag between me and the webbing and knelt on the floor with my bum on the air, thinking what an inglorious position this was in which to die. I tested my position and figured I would break my neck on impact, but that was better than burning alive, so I left it at that. Everyone seemed to be busy sorting out the softest of their possessions and manoeuvring for position.

I had noticed we were circling in smaller spirals now and got up to look out the window. Saigon was closer, the lights burned brightly below. I thought of the girls waiting all these hours at the airport, knowing our plane was in trouble and worrying themselves sick. I hoped they would watch the landing and, if we crashed, be able to tell my parents I died bravely.

The rest happened quickly. The crewman appeared, blew three shrill blasts on his whistle and disappeared back into the dark cockpit. The lights on the plane went out and I took my position. I had chosen to lie in the tail of the plane, having heard somewhere that this was the safest place to be in a crashlanding. I was right next to the Medivac patient and his nurse did not take emergency procedures for herself, but steeled the stretcher and tied down the drip stand. She removed the bottle and held it high in her hand. She looked across at me and said, 'And I thought *this boy* needed help!' Then her lips moved silently and I guessed she was praying.

'Holly, girl,' I said to myself, 'only the good die young.'

We touched down with a squeal of rubber and a violent wrenching. The plane slid sideways down the runway. Once on the ground, I leapt up and moved over the prostrate bodies to the nearest window. Fire trucks and ambulances, sirens blaring (a typical Yank touch, I thought), were keeping pace with us down the runway, which had a thick layer of foam over it. The plane finally stopped, facing the way we had come, and the soldiers at the back were first out the door, assisting the nurse with the stretcher patient. The poor man had died and the nurse stood up from examining him with tears running down her face. Her god hadn't heard her.

I was lifted down by strong arms and carried through the muck on the runway to an ambulance. When it was full, we were driven back to the terminal.

It was close to midnight and the girls were still there, rushing towards me and crying with relief. They had rounded up General Joseph's aide with the big black limousine and they took me back to the General's quarters for my R and R.

The General was in Bangkok with his wife for the weekend, so we had the place to ourselves. Yuk, the General's beagle, licked me all over, whimpering. She was a silly animal, but loved me, and I was the only one who could call her to heel with any show of obedience. Bob, one of the General's boys, had food ready to cook and we fell on dinner after several drinks. I slept that night in General Joseph's bed — I felt I deserved it after what I had just been through. Yuk slept with me.

By the time I awoke on Sunday, it was late afternoon and I just had time to shower and catch a flight back up to Cam Ranh. My weekend was lost, thanks to the VC, whose aim seemed to be getting better of late. Maybe they were practising more, I thought.

Penny, Kerry and Gail came back to the airport and waved me off. I kissed Penny goodbye, as she had thrown in the towel and was returning to Australia the next weekend. She had become so much a part of my life that I thought the war might end now that she was leaving. I couldn't imagine Vietnam without her.

'No, Holly,' she replied, when I asked her to extend for another six months, 'I've got enough money saved now for a trip around the world, or two, and I'm not going to push my luck.'

Back at Cam Ranh, my roommate Anna met me with a borrowed jeep and we drove back to the Mini Court, she clucking as I told her about the crashlanding. She was a kindly, down-to-earth girl, very straight and honest, and she didn't like Vietnam very much. She could not understand why I loved it so, loved being there, loved my Vietnamese workers and the whole way of life there. All she wanted to do was to earn her money, save as much as she could and complete her 12-month stint without having to acknowledge that there was a war on, if possible.

Jeff was waiting in the trailer. He and Anna had become great mates and spent a lot of time together at Market Time.

We ate dinner, then Jeff started talking about his coming departure from the country. He had done his 12 months and was due to go home in September. He said there was no chance of his staying on a further six months. I felt that night as if I was being deserted by all my buddies.

'Cheer up, matey,' Jeff said. 'Come on, hop in the jeep and we'll all go down to the CPO's club and take some of their money.'

Anna wasn't too happy about Jeff's gambling, but I was. I was lucky or clever at cards, I wasn't sure which. When I played poker, I did not drink. I figured that was how I could beat the chiefs, and it worked.

When we rolled into the clubhouse, the place was in full swing. We pulled chairs up to a poker game and were dealt in. Anna just sat and watched.

By 9pm, Jeff and I had cleaned out every Yank who wanted to play with us, when in came two toughies, ready to play cards. Jeff winked at me.

'You want a vehicle?' he said in a low voice across the table. 'Well, now's your chance.'

He went over to the bar and started talking to the two chiefs, hands waggling and head shaking. The three of them came to the table and took their seats, one chief rifling the cards in a very professional manner.

'What's the game and stakes?' he asked me.

'Dealer's choice and a jeep,' I replied quickly.

He thought about it, frowning.

'No way the jeep,' he said, 'but how about a 21-cubic-foot freezer?'

I accepted, and the cards were dealt.

I bet $300 against the freezer — and won.

Another round was dealt, the stakes this time rose to a $2,400 pot in the centre of the table. I won again. I figured Jeff was letting me win, as he folded each time after pushing up the stakes for me.

'Cleans me out,' said one chief.

'Finishes me too,' said the other.

'Come on,' I wheedled, as they drained their glasses, 'one more hand and one more drink. For your jeep.'

They hesitated for a moment and Jeff said loudly, 'Perhaps they just can't play poker like they do in the movies.'

'You're on!' said the first chief, and I dealt.

I couldn't believe my hand. I had the 10, jack, queen and ace of hearts, and the 10 of spades. I was glad Anna had no idea how to play cards, as she was perched on the arm of my chair, looking over my shoulder, and her face never changed. The chiefs were watching her look at my cards and they placed their bets. I raised and asked for one card. I could see them thinking, 'She's going for a straight — outside chance' and then the key to the jeep was thrown in the pot.

I picked up my dealt card, saying 'Dealer takes one,' as I did. I dared not look at it. I so desperately wanted that jeep.

I composed my face, then brought my card up to join the others in my hand. It fitted nicely in between the queen and the ace — it was the king of hearts — my favourite man.

I resisted the terrible urge to place it in its rightful order in my hand, leaving it jutting out the end of my fan of cards, trying to look slightly rattled.

The chief on my left bet $300, the minimum stake. Jeff folded. The chief on my right indicated the jeep key, shining among the paper money on the table, saying 'That's my bet, for whatever it's worth.'

I carefully counted out $300, resisted the temptation to push the stakes up for fear of scaring them off. I wanted to see their faces when I laid my hand down. 'I'll see you,' I told the fellow on the left.

'Three deuces,' he laid his cards down.

'Ha!' shouted the chief on my right. 'Three fours.'

He reached out to gather in the pot.

'Just a minute, I think I might have won that,' I said, and laid down my beautiful Royal Flush. My heart was thumping and my hands were weak and shaky. I thought he might accuse me of cheating, it was such a lucky hand.

Jeff was leaning back in his seat, twirling his gun around on his finger, cigar stuck in the corner of his teeth. The chiefs looked at him, and at me, and said, 'Great hand, little lady, great hand.'

I collected my money and the ignition key and the padlock key for the jeep, then we all went outside so that the chiefs could show me which vehicle I had won. It was a nice navy grey one, good upholstery, with a holding bar across the top. I liked it! Jeff took the keys and hopped in for a ride and, showing off, did a fast U-turn in front of the club and fell out and broke his shoulder bone. He rode home in the ambulance and Anna and I rode home in our new jeep.

The freezer was delivered on a two and a half tonne truck the next day. I stayed home from work to take delivery and they had to take the door off the trailer to get it in. It was huge — but empty. I hadn't thought about where to get food to fill it and realised I had probably won a white elephant.

I went to see a mess sergeant who owed me a favour for getting him some Aussie beer and he took me down to the big wooden buildings near the docks and into the cold storage rooms. The walls were lined with boxes of goodies — steaks (finest fillet), bacon, fresh eggs and other perishable food. I selected a case each of steak, bacon and eggs and drove home, struggling to carry each case up the trailer steps and into the freezer.

'Happiness is a *full* freezer,' I said to myself and set off again in the jeep to the wharves. I sat for a while watching the loading and unloading of the ships. A chopper hovered above a pallet of food boxes and figures ran underneath to hook the pallet on the chopper which swung up and away with its load. An idea formed in my head.

I turned about and drove to Teeny Weeny Airport, but there were no choppers there. So I drove the 20km over the bridge to Dong Ba Thin village and out to the chopper base there. Charlie, a long-time friend, listened to my plan and grinned. He rounded up another two guys and we climbed aboard a Huey chopper and headed off to the docks.

We circled a while, trying to read the printing on the boxes on the wharves and settled on a pallet that looked like it held a variety of goods. Charlie hovered over it. Sure enough, figures ran underneath us and hooked us up to the pallet. Laughing hysterically, we flew away with our stolen goods, back to Dong Ba Thin to count our grab. I split with the boys and drove home with another six cases of canned goods, including cakes and pastries. Yum.

Word soon spread around the Mini Court that Trailer B6 had a freezer and the food started rolling in. Guys turned up with all sorts of goodies; the general's aide brought two cases of lobster tails and we had a 'clambake' down by Tiger Lake. From then on, our trailer was the cordon bleu restaurant of Cam Ranh Bay. People used our freezer to store their stolen food and split us for the eats. I even had the temerity to invite General Seagrove to dinner, dishing up food to him that had been stolen from his own ration. If he noticed, he didn't comment.

He did comment, though, about how he found great difficulty in getting a helicopter available to him for official flights, but I seemed to be able to crook my little finger and have one immediately.

'Privileges of rank, Sir,' I told him, my nose in the air.

'And, while we're on the subject, young lady,' he scolded me, 'can you please tell your pilot friends to stop buzzing your office when they come home from a flight. It's noisy, apart from dangerous.'

I promised I would and I also promised I would use a proper airport in future when directing a chopper where to put me down on the army base. I had found it quicker and easier in the mornings, if I had slept over at any of the bases across the bay, to have the pilots drop me at the 92nd finance building, right in the middle of the camp. It always gave the soldiers a fright when a helicopter landed right in the middle of their drill area and they had to scatter to make way for it. The officers weren't too happy either to see me jump out, crying 'Thanks fellas' and run off to work.

A couple of weeks after winning my jeep, two army MPs came and took it away. They stripped the engine and found that its engine number coincided with a stolen army jeep, so they confiscated it. 'Bloody navy,' I thought. So I was back to square one on the transport problem. What I needed was my own helicopter, or my own private pilot, or something.

I was pondering these seemingly insurmountable problems on the morning of 11 August 1969, which dawned just like any other day, but suddenly, C-Day was thrust on me.

Chapter Fourteen

THREE GUESSES WHERE THE MONEY WENT!

THE FIRST THING I noticed when I entered the quonset hut Personnel Office was that there were no Vietnamese at work. In fact, none were in sight on the base and the PX store was closed too.

All the snack bars and mess halls were closed immediately after breakfast and big trucks with armed guards rolled into the base, pulling up at 92nd finance. They carried huge padlocked metal trunks into the building and the doors were locked behind them.

My boss told me it was C-Day, or Conversion Day. I knew from October 1968 what that meant! A day of being locked in, waiting my turn to change my Military Payment Certificates (MPC) into the new issue of currency. C-Day was sprung on us so that we would have no idea of its imminence and therefore have no time to organise the changing of illegally gotten gains. When the tallies had been made after the last C-Day, the grand sum of $6 million was outstanding. I wondered how much this day would do to cancel out the flow of American dollars.

The Vietnamese were allowed to own and use only their own currency, piastres. All other people in the country were allowed to own and use MPC. We were paid by cheque after allotments had been made to our banks in America and we could cash our cheques in the finance section at work into MPC. Then, if we wanted to spend any of that money in the local economy, we could change a portion of it into piastres. This is where the black market came in. If we cashed MPC illegally with Viet or Indian money changers, we could get sometimes twice as much in piastres for each dollar changed. 'Green' or US currency was strictly forbidden in-country. All monetary exchanges between the non-Vietnamese communities was done in MPC, and with Viets in piastres. To even own green in any quantity was punishable by court-martial. When leaving the country on termination of employment, one could change a certain amount only into green and only with letters of authority and on production of exit visas or travel orders.

C-Day was designed to outwit the black marketeers. Those who had collected large sums and, by large sums we are talking about hundreds of thousands of dollars, in black market transactions and hoarded it (it could not be banked without explanation), were suddenly confronted with the prospect of being able to change only $150 into the new currency — the rest of their money after C-Day would be utterly useless, no better than Monopoly money. They might as well have burnt it.

If one had more that $150 to change over (and I had $800 from a poker game the previous week), witnesses had to be called and good reasons given to gain permission to change over more than the allowed amount. I knew I was in for a hell of a day.

Hours later, my turn came to see the commander and request my specified amount to convert. I handed over close to $1,000 and his eyebrows shot up. At my request, he rang Market Time and spoke with the two very disgruntled chiefs, who told him of my poker win, and I was allowed to convert $987 into the new currency. I was starving and left the finance building to search for lunch. Without Viet staff, the mess halls were not functioning properly and the line was too long, so Jeff, Anna and I decided we should go across to the village for some Korean food.

At the gate to the bridge there were dozens of Viets with big baskets of money, old MPC notes stuffed into bags, all crying out to any passer-by to change some money for them. I felt a little sorry for them; some had their life savings tied up in the now worthless currency. But the Filipinos were the funniest sight. One told me he had made $8,000 in four days by stealing steaks, hairspray and washing powder, and now he was stuck with $8,000 worth of useless paper money. Like us, he could personally change only $150 unless he could show where the rest came from. It was the Korean soldiers, the Filipinos and the Thais who conducted most of the black marketeering; this was quite obvious by the paltry amounts the Vietnamese wanted us to exchange for them. I remembered doing a 'spot search' of female Vietnamese employees at an upcountry PX store. That particular store had an inventory variance in three months of more than $151,000 due to pilferage. Being the only female PX employee on base who was not Vietnamese, I was directed to do a complete body search of the staff, which was sprung on them without warning. I checked bras and pants, umbrellas, shoes and in long hair piled up on heads. Apart from three loose cigarettes down the front of one old lady's brassiere, I did not find one item of PX goods on those girls. The store manager was a Filipino and, after I had made my report to security branch, a closer watch was kept on him and finally he was caught in his Vietnamese girlfriend's house in the village with more than $100,000 worth of stolen PX goods. I didn't feel at all sorry for the other Third Country Nationals on C-Day.

That afternoon, my boss told me I was being sent on TDY to a village called Ban Me Thuot, far to the west near the Cambodian border. There was a PX store there and I was to assist in the C-Day changeover, and also to check out the civilian staff there to see if all was well. I took a jeep and went home to pack my little Pan Am bag with fresh clothing and my ID and ration cards, as I figured I would be spending the night there. Back at the office, my boss told me to take Rudy, one of the Filipinos from the Personnel Branch, with me to assist. He also handed me his .357 Magnum pistol.

'There have been VC offensives in the area and you might need this,' he said and showed me how to work it. I put the safety catch on, checked that it was loaded and stuck it in my shoulder holster under my fatigue jacket where it could not be seen. It was illegal for a civilian to carry a weapon, but I would rather break the law than be dead.

We were driven to the Cam Ranh air terminal and loaded onto a C-7A, which flew us to Dalat in the central highlands. There we boarded a KIA (killed in action) flight and sat for the remainder of the trip to Ban Me Thuot trying not to gag on the smell. Poor Rudy was quite sick.

By the time we landed and had walked to the main village, the PX store was closed so we could not do our job until the next day. We were therefore unable to assist in the currency conversion and I just hoped that it had been conducted properly and that no store managers or employees had been able to talk their way into changing any illegally obtained funds. I put checking this with the finance branch on the top of my list of things to do in the morning.

Rudy and I found our way to the only hotel in town and took a shared room with twin beds. We could charge two rooms and split the difference between us for the other room when we collected our travel pay back at Cam Ranh Bay. We had a room on the upper floor of the hotel, at the opposite end of the corridor to where the stairs were. It was the usual Vietnamese hotel room, with wooden beds, each with a thin rubber mattress and worn sheets on it. No hot water. No airconditioner. No glass in the windows. And it cost $30 for one night.

'What the hell,' I said to Rudy. 'Let's go downstairs and see about some eats.'

Downstairs the town was silent. It was an ominous quiet. I could not quite put my finger on the reason, but thought it might have been due to the discontent of the locals over C-Day. No Viets in the street smiled or nodded to us; there were no groups sitting at sidewalk cafes talking and laughing. There were no children in sight.

The few soldiers we saw looked at us curiously, but none stopped to talk. I began to feel very uneasy and suggested to Rudy that we just buy some French loaves and dried fish and eat in our room. He nodded, also feeling the strange mood of the town. It was like the quiet and stillness before an electrical storm.

We were sitting on our beds, eating our bread rolls, when all hell broke loose in the street below. Shouting and the sound of gunfire reached us first, then loud explosions punctuated the night. A grenade was lobbed into the hotel foyer downstairs and the entire building shook with the deafening explosion. I could hear the sound of falling timber long after the explosion died away.

Rudy and I looked at each other and he burst into tears. He blubbered and cried and ran around in circles.

'Jesus,' I thought, 'I've got to look after *him* too.'

He was utterly useless, a quivering heap of humanity.

'Just stay here,' I commanded him, making my voice stern.

He nodded helplessly and I opened the door cautiously and looked down the corridor. Smoke was curling up the stairs. The hotel was on fire.

I turned back to Rudy. 'We've got to get out of this place,' I told him. He just nodded, still crying.

I got out the .357 Magnum and checked it, taking off the safety catch. I grabbed the mattresses off the beds and placed one around Rudy's shoulders like a shawl. I did the same with the other, hoisting it high over my head to afford the best protection possible. Then, with the gun in front and Rudy on my heels, we proceeded to the top of the stairs.

I peered down. The place was full of smoke and twisted wood. The stairs ended halfway down, smashed to fragments by the grenade. Beckoning Rudy, I tentatively tried each step on the way down. Rocking on the last solid step, I judged my distance, then jumped to the ground floor. Rudy followed doggedly. Flames were licking up the walls and across the floor and a bare foot was lying charred among the debris. My mind clicked shut against it. 'I've got to get out. I've got to get out,' I repeated to myself.

Stumbling over twisted and broken chairs and pot plants, I poked my head out and looked quickly up and down the street. It was deserted. To my right, about 180 metres away at the end of the street, I could see the MACV compound and, behind the wire, I could make out a Huey chopper, blades swirling slowly, working up towards a take-off.

'Run for the chopper,' I whispered urgently to Rudy, pointing it out to him. He hesitated, but when I leapt out into the street and started sprinting towards the chopper, he was galvanised into action and overtook me in his fear. There was one side street between us and the compound, off to our right. Rudy shot across the cross street and, as I puffed up the road behind him, a Viet in black satin pants and no shirt, with a rifle held across his chest, jumped out after him and swung the rifle around to take aim at Rudy's fast-disappearing back. I lifted my pistol and shot him at close range right in the middle of his back. He disintegrated before my eyes, his rifle flying up the road past a startled Rudy, who stopped and looked back. It seemed to take an age for the dismembered lower half of the body to fall to the ground. I watched in horror as it fell slowly, then twitched and jumped around on the pavement. I didn't know what happened to his top half. It just disappeared when I shot him.

Rudy screamed and I leapt over the black satin legs and, pushing Rudy ahead of me, ran to the compound gates. They were open and a guard's head popped up out of the pillbox with a startled expression. We didn't stop, just raced towards the chopper, fear driving us both to tremendous speeds.

The Huey was just lifting off the ground as Rudy reached it. He frantically tried to catch the attention of the crew, grabbing at legs and seats. He grabbed the barrel of the gunner's rifle and swung on it. He was lucky he wasn't shot at again!

The guys pulled us both aboard and we sank to the floor across their feet as the chopper took off. Rudy was babbling and I was crying hysterically, waving the .357

Magnum around in my distress. A firm hand encircled my
wrist and the gun was removed from my fingers. Then two
strong arms hauled me off the floor and onto a lap.

'Hey, hey,' the soldier smoothed my hair back and
wiped my tears away with his jacket sleeve. 'You're safe now,
you're safe.'

I quietened down, but Rudy was still rocking the boat,
bawling and shivering with fear.

'Tell your friend there,' the soldier shouted in my ear,
'that if he doesn't quieten down, he can take a walk down to
the ground.'

I grabbed Rudy and pulled him up into a sitting
position. He rolled his eyes at me. He was terrified of the
chopper, as well as by the events at Ban Me Thuot, and it
took a rabbit chop by one of the crew to settle him down for
the trip to Dalat.

By the time we reached Cam Ranh Bay airfield, it was
the middle of the next day. We had slept in any empty plane
at Dalat, then sat on the flight lines for hours waiting for a
flight that was going home. We travelled back with the
wounded from the attack on Ban Me Thuot, and all the
while I was counting my lucky stars that neither Rudy nor
I was among them. I spent most of the flight drumming into
Rudy's head that he must never mention that I had a gun
with me and giving him millions of reasons for keeping quiet,
including the promise of $300 in new currency.

Back at Cam Ranh, I made my report to my boss,
leaving out certain facts, then went home to my trailer for a

long, cool bath and a rest. I was still feeling weak from my experience and when I lay down to sleep, I kept seeing that awful twitching trunk sinking slowly to the pavement.

I told Anna about it in detail when she came home from work and repeated it again to Jeff when he came in later.

'What you need is some fun to cheer you up,' said Jeff, and he suggested we drive to the air base to see the Australian entertainer, Tassie Hamilton, whose show was on at the officers' mess that night.

I had wanted to see Tassie's show since the Catholic chaplain had banned it. He was a creep and I figured that if he hated it, it was bound to be terrific. Colonel Garcia had overridden his objections and the show was booked. When we arrived, the mess hall was packed to capacity and we had to stand at the back.

Tassie Hamilton strode out onto the stage. She was Australia's answer to Phyllis Diller — only better, I thought. She looked around the room at the sea of faces, and said, 'So you guys think you're the only ones to see a war?' Then she proceeded to tell us about the 'war to end all wars', World War II, and the Korean War, singing songs and telling jokes applicable to each era. She sang *Lily Marlene, Mademoiselle from Armitiers, Pack up Your Troubles, It's a Long Way to Tipperary* ... then all the rude versions. She spotted the Catholic chaplain sitting in the front row (he came only to be able to condemn her show firsthand), and she jumped from the stage and sidled up to him, leering lecherously at him and laughing at his embarrassment. Then, quick as a wink, she whipped her T-shirt up and over his bald pink head, boxing his ears underneath the shirt with her ample boobs. We all screamed with delight and cheered and, when she finally let his head see light again, she asked, with great concern, 'Can you breathe better now, dearie?' She patted his pate, then offered him a comb. I was nearly falling on the floor with laughter.

Then she sang all the songs we would always associate with the Vietnam War: *We've Gotta Get Outta This Place*, *House of the Rising Sun*, *Hey Jude*, *Good Morning Starshine* and more. She talked about Australia and of the number of Americans who went on R and R to Sydney and how they all loved it. Then she sang songs that made my heart ache with homesickness: *The Road to Gundagai*, *Click Go the Shears*, *Botany Bay* and, of course, *Waltzing Matilda*. I stood up the back of the room with tears streaming down my face, holding Jeff's arm, completely lost in the moment.

'Don't tell me we have another Aussie in this goddamn place,' she cried, stopping in the middle of a song.

'Yes, yes,' shouted the guys, turning to point at me.

'Well, come on up here and I'll sing you a special song,' Tassie said. Jeff nudged me forward. I made my way to the stage and she took my hand and said, 'At last, Australia has a national song, and I am proud to be the first one to sing it to you.'

She launched into *God Bless Australia*, to the tune of *Waltzing Matilda*, holding my hands and looking into my eyes as she sang. Out of respect, the entire room stood to attention while she lifted her voice and carried the beautiful song over the hushed crowd.

> *God bless Australia,*
> *God bless Australia,*
> *Land of the Anzacs, the brave and the free.*
> *It's our own land, our homeland,*
> *From now until eternity,*
> *God bless Australia, the land of the free.*

I bawled unashamedly on the stage, she kissed me when the song was finished and I made my way back to Jeff and Anna. The day had just been too much for me. Suddenly, I needed desperately to go home, to see my parents and family again. I resolved that re-entry visa or not, I would go home before Christmas and get back into Vietnam somehow.

The next day Jeff and I boarded a flight to Saigon. He had decided he had had enough of war and was going to make arrangements to resign and go home to Sydney. I was going down to demand the 30-day leave due to me. I had already forfeited one home leave and this time I was determined I was not going to take no for an answer. It had been two years since I had seen my folks and, although I wasn't ready to leave Vietnam permanently yet, I was bloody well going to have a month away from the place to rest and recuperate.

Chapter Fifteen

HOME AND HOSED

JEFF AND I flew to Saigon and I took him to the girls' house to stay. Gail and Kerry were wild with excitement to see me and blew up air mattresses for Jeff and me to sleep on. It was Saturday and the girls decided to take a sickie from work so that we could spend more time together.

'Never let it be said that I let a work day interfere with my social obligations,' said Kerry, smirking as she broke open a bottle of bourbon.

There was a party at Phu Loi that night, but the girls all had dates in Saigon and were not attending. Jeff and I rolled along with them, making a party of six. We went to our favourite Mayfair Restaurant and then to a Vietnamese nightclub, which was pretty boring, as no dancing was allowed. We all went home early, feeling a little let down.

'If we get up early enough,' suggested Gail, 'we can try to pick up a chopper at Tan San Nhut and still make it to Phu Loi for lunch.'

We agreed enthusiastically and, in the morning, we set off in taxis to the PX headquarters to try to get a vehicle and driver to take us out to the airport. Chantou was at the office, putting in some overtime and, at our insistence, said she would also come to Phu Loi.

Buz, one of the American civilian workers, said he would accompany us to the airport and drive the PX van back afterwards. So we all piled in — Buz in the driver's seat and me beside him. Kerry and Gail in the second seat and Jeff in the middle of the back seat with Chantou next to him.

We were sitting in a traffic jam less than 200 metres from the airport checkpoint, when a cocky little White Mouse holding a large rifle strutted up to the van and waved his rifle at Chantou, shouting at her in Vietnamese. She answered him derisively. He grew angry and raised his rifle above his head, firing off a shot. Before we could drive off, we were surrounded by White Mice, all brandishing pistols and rifles at us.

Jeff tried to get out of the vehicle, but was pushed back by a Mouse. The same policeman grabbed Chantou's arm and dragged her out onto the street. She stood up, still talking fast to him, and produced her ID card, which he promptly pocketed without examining. I was furious. I started to yell at him, but Chantou said, 'He's just mad because I am sitting next to a white man.'

'Tell him I never saw you till half an hour ago,' said Jeff.

'They want lots of money to let us go,' Chantou translated.

'Never,' we all said together.

So we sat, and sat, and sat. We sat in that vehicle surrounded by crummy little White Mice from 8.30am to 2pm, under armed guard. Finally some American MPs came by (they seemed to be everywhere when they weren't wanted, but this day when we needed one desperately, it was more than five hours before we saw one). The MPs assessed the situation quickly and demanded that we be allowed to pass. The White Mouse who had the number '512' printed on his cap said in broken English that we could go, but Chantou had to stay.

Chantou told us to go, her eyes begging us to get help. So we locked up the vehicle and, leaving Buz and Jeff to stay with Chantou, we girls got the MPs to drive us to General Joseph's quarters on the other side of the airport. Gail voiced all our thoughts when she said, 'Bloody little racist pig.' We were determined to do something about it, to have the damn Mice exposed to the head of police for attempted bribery and for harassment, particularly of foreigners. But the General was away for the weekend, as usual, so our hopes of taking the situation to the highest authority in the military were dashed. His aide, Bob, however, and several other soldiers attached to the General's staff, drove us back to the parked van to see if they could help Chantou.

Jeff and Buz were sitting alone in the van. They told us Chantou had been taken away, protesting violently, and that they had been powerless to do anything because every time one of them made a move to assist her, rifles were prodded into their backs. And they weren't about to argue with loaded rifles.

'Do you have any idea which precinct the Mice were from?' asked Bob.

I remembered seeing '512' on the cap of one of them and told him so.

'Right,' he said. 'That station is over behind the General's house. Let's go!'

We climbed back into the General's big black limousine and drove through back streets to the Precinct 512 jailhouse. We must have been an impressive mob, all striding into the little reception room, faces grim. Apart from us three girls, there was Jeff and Buz, three MACV army officers and two military policemen. Bob immediately thumped the desk, startling the White Mouse who was sitting behind it. Although he couldn't understand Bob's request, one look at our faces and he knew we meant business. He scurried away into the back rooms.

Bob followed closely on his heels and we all raced after him. We went down a corridor past what seemed to be offices on each side and into the lockup at the rear of the building. There was Chantou, flat on her back on a dirty cot, locked in a barred jail room, her eyes bruised, her mouth bleeding and completely naked. She pushed the Viet policeman who was raping her off and ran to the bars when she saw us, weeping silently.

The entire police station was alive with movement. The receptionist guy unlocked the cell with shaking hands.

The Mouse in the cell with Chantou tried to put on his trousers, but one of the American MPs raced in and punched him in the face, splattering blood and teeth across the wall. Chantou stumbled out and we girls crowded around her, trying to comfort her and cover her nakedness. White Mice were evacuating the place as if it was on fire and our boys were chasing them, pulling them down with football tackles and smashing into their faces without mercy.

We wrapped Chantou in a dirty sheet from the cot and took her to the car. The boys joined us and we drove back to the General's house, where his little Viet maid clucked over Chantou, washed her and fed her. She was then put to bed between clean sheets, with a couple of sleeping tablets. All she could say to me, as I held her hand as she drifted off into sleep, was, 'No worry, Holly, no worry too much about it. Happens all the time, no worry ...'

We had dinner and the boys promised they would bring this episode to the attention of General Joseph. I truly hoped they would. The arrogance and blatant corruption of the Vietnamese Police Force had always rankled me. If citizens could not turn to their police as protectors, then society was sick indeed.

After a distressing and wasted Sunday, Jeff and I set off for the Cholon PX headquarters on Monday to see what could be done about some respite for me and termination of employment for him. We filled out our respective application forms in the Personnel Branch, in quadruplicate with forms C, D and XYZ or whatever, and a prissy little know-it-all

Filipina checked them through, made me rewrite mine about five times, then said, 'Come back at four to see the Personnel Officer.'

Jeff took the opportunity to go to Third Field Hospital to have his collarbone checked out and emerged some time later to where I was waiting in the casualty section, grinning and waving his arm, which was now free of the sling.

'I was hoping to go home with bandages, looking like a real veteran,' he said.

'Oh you're a real vet all right,' I told him, thinking of his prowess at poker.

Back at the office, Jeff went in to see the Chief of Personnel first. His interview took only 10 minutes, and he emerged happily to tell me he was rotating (going home) mid-September.

'Try to see if you can get on the same flight and we'll have some fun in Bangkok and Singapore,' he said.

My interview was shorter. I was told I could leave, there would be no problem getting me an exit visa, but there was also no chance of obtaining a re-entry visa for me. I had a choice. I could stay on and miss another home leave, or I could leave, take all my things with me in case I couldn't get back, but attempt to get an entry visa in Sydney or in Bangkok. I was given three minutes to weigh up the alternatives. Maybe I would have opted to stay if I hadn't seen what had happened to Chantou the previous day, but I was truly homesick and I thought, 'if I can't get back, so what?' So I told the Chief of Personnel to make up my travel orders and organise my exit visa, banking and currency authorities, bookings and hotel reservations to coincide with Jeff's. Then Jeff and I went downtown to Saigon and drank ourselves into a stupor to celebrate or commiserate, as the case may have been.

We took the late flight back to Cam Ranh Bay and rang Anna to collect us from the airport. She arrived in Jeff's jeep, her face anxious. When Jeff told her he was definitely leaving, her composure broke and she cried. I had never realised until then just how attached she was to Jeff. They always did things together, but I had looked on their friendship as that of brother and sister. It was obviously more than that.

'How short are you?' she asked, almost afraid of the answer.

'Eighteen and a wake-up,' he replied, meaning 18 more full days and he would leave on the 19th.

'Me, too,' I cried, trying to cheer her up, 'only, mark my words, I'll be back!'

'Fat chance,' she said glumly. 'I'll not survive here alone without you two. The place will be like a morgue.'

'You'll survive,' said Jeff, quietly and seriously to her. 'And then you'll complete your contract and come to Australia and marry me.'

'If I live that long,' she replied, then shrugged off her unhappiness in her characteristic, practical way and suggested we eat out at the Army Officers' Mess. 'They have lobster tonight.'

The next day I processed Jeff and myself as terminating staff, but I told my boss I would be back.

'I don't like your chances,' he replied.

The morning of our departure arrived and Jeff and I had terrible hangovers from our farewell parties. I told everyone I would be back, but no one believed me. Anna was bequeathed Jeff's jeep and she drove us to the airport at 6am in the cold morning air. Halfway there, I offered to drive and Anna and Jeff cuddled and whispered and cried in the back seat.

Farewells were swift. Outgoing travel orders always acted like magic on the airport booking staff and Jeff and I were allotted seats on the first flight out. Everyone kissed us and shook our hands. Anna stood on the runway and waved her scarf until the plane was out of sight.

'Are you really going to marry her?' I asked him when we were airborne.

'Too right,' he replied. 'I'll start divorce proceedings from my wife the minute I set foot in Sydney.' He fell into deep thought.

'Christ,' I thought to myself, 'what's this war doing to us all?' We had all become insular, totally wrapped up in a cocoon called the Vietnam War. The real world was far away and totally unimportant. Any friends I had before the war were no longer friends, simply because they could not possibly comprehend what we had been through. I pitied the returning soldier. I had read somewhere a funny piece called 'Handle him with care', in which advice was given to the wives of returnees. 'Ignore him if he drinks his soup out of his helmet,' it said. 'If he falls to the pavement when a car backfires, try to understand.' It was written tongue-in-cheek, but I wondered just how true it might be.

In Saigon, we attended our out-processing at Personnel Branch and, clutching passports (I hadn't seen mine for nearly two years) and authorisations, we made our way to the girls' house where we would stay the night. Our flight was due to depart at Tan San Nhut commercial airport at 10am the next day.

It was a quiet last evening in Saigon. Gail announced that she thought she would call it quits too, but I talked her into staying on for at least another five weeks, just to see if I made it back into the country. If I succeeded, the way was open for us all to take home leave. She agreed.

I was nervous at the airport. The immigration officer, a Vietnamese, checked my passport photo by holding it next to my face. He counted my money twice. He rifled through my baggage (one suitcase) and through Jeff's too. At last we were told we could board that big Freedom Bird, and we turned and kissed the girls then rushed for the plane, laughing and skipping like kids let out of school.

On the Thai International flight I was handed an orchid and a fan by the hostess. We were given free drinks all the way to Bangkok, a compliment given to all people boarding at Saigon, the hostess told us. We had been the only two leaving that day. I thought it was hardly worth the airline's stopover, but was glad they thought it was!

We didn't stop in Bangkok, just hung around the airport until 4pm when we boarded our Qantas flight bound for Sydney via Singapore.

Oh, beautiful, beautiful Qantas. I ate three helpings of green peas. Jeff doubled up on fillet mignon, and we both gorged ourselves on desserts. The stewards were wonderful as we told them we were coming from Saigon and were going home. They made our trip memorable, with kindness and free drinks. And with no-nonsense Aussie care.

The next morning, the sun rose over the Australian desert, red and gold below us. We had gone through immigration in Darwin in the early hours of the morning, had breakfasted and the plane buzzed with that lovely pre-landing anticipation as the stewards rushed to and fro, readying us to depart from their hands.

As we circled over Botany Bay and came in to land from the east, my throat gummed up and tears rushed down my face. Jeff squeezed my hand. We had no words to say to each other. We knew what we were both feeling at that moment.

We said goodbye to each other at the customs shed, he promising to write, and I promising to look out for Anna when I returned. Then I saw my parents and ran to them, joy filling my whole being. I had no idea that I had missed the safe, wonderful security of home so much.

But, after a week at home, having reunions with former workmates and friends, I was bored to tears. I could not sleep at night (it was *too quiet*); I swivelled every time

I saw a rare Asian face in the streets; life was no longer *urgent* — I wasn't where *it* was happening. I itched and ached to be back in the middle of the war again. Stupid politicians were having anti-Vietnam demonstrations and marches in the streets, shouting support for the National Liberation Front. I wanted to stand up and shout at them, 'Have you *been* there? Don't talk about what you know nothing about.' I was furious that they presented only a very minor side of the war to the public in Australia. I wanted to tell them about my Viet friends, their homes and dreams, their aspirations and hopes, and how they all wanted us to help them prevent a foreign power taking over their country. But what use was one voice against the multitude?

I felt like a fish out of water, flapping hopelessly in an alien world. The rounds of parties I had attended and thought exciting before Vietnam were now shallow and boring. The men looked insipid and pallid. Was it because they didn't wear uniforms, I thought? I studied faces at parties, trying to figure out how that man would look in a uniform, or how this one would look in an officer's cap. But it definitely wasn't the uniform that was missing. There was something indefinable about men at war that was exciting. A sort of *secretive* power, as though soldiers knew more about the core of existence than an ordinary businessman. These civilians didn't laugh so hard, or play so hard, or work so hard as the military men. They seemed sluggish compared with their counterparts in Vietnam.

'How was Vietnam?' they all asked me.

How could I possibly explain? If I had tried, they would not have understood anyway. So I just said 'fine' and left it at that.

Their half-hearted attempts to flirt with me were insipid and hopeless. I longed for my suntanned, tall, virile Yankees back there in the war.

I booked my fare with Qantas to Singapore, allowing myself a two-day stopover to see the place. My connecting flight was with Pan American to Bangkok and I had a return ticket to Sydney. I took a 14-day visa for Bangkok.

Once there, I petitioned the Embassy of the Republic of South Vietnam for an entry visa, but one look at my passport produced a firm refusal. I then went to the Australian Embassy and told them I had lost my passport and requested a new one. This took several days and my entry visa to Bangkok was incorporated in the new passport. I then reapplied to the South Vietnamese Embassy for an entry visa, but this time was given a three-day stopover visa only. It seemed I would have no way to stay in the country of my choice. I booked my flight to Saigon on Cathay Pacific and boarded, trying to look as though it was my first visit to the country. I had no plan in my head, but knew only that I didn't want to let the Viet officialdom know I had returned.

When the plane landed at Tan San Nhut, I exited from the rear of the plane and hung back a little as I watched the few other disembarking passengers straggle over the tarmac towards the terminal entrance. I was standing in the shade of the tail when, from across the runway, a voice hailed me by name. I turned to see Chuck running towards me from the military hangars and suddenly it was clear what I should do.

'Write off your clothing,' I told myself, hoisting my cabin bag and camera over my shoulder and running off to meet Chuck. The plane effectively hid me from the terminal entrance.

I met him midway across the runway and we raced flat out to the other side, hoping all the while that no jet would land and flatten us.

'Welcome back,' Chuck puffed. 'We all bet that you wouldn't make it home and back.'

'I'm not back yet,' I said, looking over my shoulder. I need not have worried. No one missed me and I just walked out of the military terminal as I had done hundreds of other times and into the Saigon streets. For sheer devilment, I walked around to the front of the commercial building and took a photograph of the terminal. When it was developed, I sent it to my parents. I wrote on the back, 'For better or for worse, I'm home and hosed.'

I was back in Vietnam and I was not going to worry about getting out again without producing an entry visa until the time came when I wanted to leave forever.

Gail, Kerry and Chantou (now recovered) were terribly excited to see me and asked immediately for news of Penny. One of the first things I had done in Sydney was to ring Penny's parents' home, but Penny was in England, spending her Vietnam savings. I hoped she felt different than

I had felt to be back in the real world. Gail had had a letter from her a few months previously and showed it to me. It was full of discontent. Penny had tried unsuccessfully to gain a re-entry visa to Vietnam and was missing us all dreadfully. I knew just how she felt.

After we had discussed the pros and cons of home leave, Gail decided she would definitely stick it out and push any homesickness aside. We all agreed it was worthwhile to stay.

I wondered if Vietnam was becoming 'home' to us and if any one of us would ever again be able to settle into a regular civilian life.

Chapter Sixteen

HAIL AND FAREWELLS

CAM RANH BAY looked no different from when I had left and neither should it have. I had been gone only a month, but it felt as though I had been to the moon and back. Anna was in the air base hospital when I returned and I went immediately to see her.

She was in a private room, much to her chagrin, and she was lonely and cranky. When I poked my head around her door and said, 'Hi, Yank', she threw aside the magazine she was reading and leapt out of bed to hug me.

'Oh, I've missed you so much,' she cried. 'I didn't eat properly, didn't drink enough liquids, and now I have a kidney complaint.'

'No one to drink with?' I chided her.

'No one like my Aussie mates,' she replied. She showed me a letter she had received from Jeff, asking her to come to Australia as quickly as possible. 'Fuck the military,' the letter said '... and assholes to your contract.'

'What can I do, Holly?' she groaned. 'I have to complete the contract or pay back the airfare.'

'Is *that* all?' I was surprised. I thought the way she was carrying on that she would have to refund salaries or something, but the airfare ... well, it was not worth thinking about.

'Hell, I'll give you the money for that,' I said.

'No, thanks, I've got enough. But do you think I ought to just chuck away my chances of working for the US Government ever again?'

'If you're going to marry Jeff and settle in Australia, what does it matter?' I asked.

She grinned at me suddenly. 'Jeff's right,' she replied, 'blah to the Government.'

She recovered rapidly and was soon back in the trailer at the Mini Court. Day by day she continued working and each night I would ask, 'Did you resign today?'

'I just don't know how to go about it,' she said. 'I heard that they can block your exit visa and make all sorts of trouble if you want to leave in the middle of a contract.'

'Leave it with me,' I replied.

I rang a friend at the US Embassy in Saigon and arranged for Anna to go down on a Saturday to see him. She returned to Cam Ranh Bay excited and thrilled. She had an exit visa, plane ticket and travel orders, all completed secretly by my friend at the embassy. All she had to do was pack her bag and let Jeff know she was coming to Australia immediately.

That presented another problem. If her departure was to remain secret, we couldn't send a cable to Jeff. We sat in the trailer on a Sunday afternoon, trying to work it out.

'We could try to ring him,' I suggested.

'How?' Anna asked. 'The only lines out of here are military and you have to have A-One priority to ring overseas. And that's General Joseph's priority.'

A gleam came into my eye. I knew the General spent nearly every weekend in Bangkok with his family. I quickly dialled his quarters' number, MACV 2635 and, sure enough, he was not at home.

'What's his priority number?' I asked Howard, his aide.

'Can't tell you that,' he said. 'What do you want to know for?'

'To get through to Clarke Air Force Base in the Philippines urgently', I replied. 'I need to speak to our Officer in Charge. He's over there playing golf and something terribly urgent has come up. All the lines out of the country are tied up on the usual Sunday personal calls to the States.'

'OK,' Howard conceded, 'but for God's sake, don't tell anyone you got it from me.'

I promised I wouldn't and he gave the priority number to me, which I copied down with a shaking hand.

I replaced the receiver and waved the paper at Anna. She was horrified.

'You can't just ring Sydney on General Joseph's number,' she cried.

'I can bloody well try!' I said, picking up the phone and dialling the Cam Ranh exchange.

They answered.

'This is Priority Alpha Two Two One Seven Nine,' I said in my best voice. 'Clear the line to Clarke for a call please.'

'Right away Ma'am,' came the reply. I winked at Anna.

The receiver crackled and buzzed. Over the humming, I heard the operator say, 'Clarke, Manila.'

'Give me Manila Commercial.' I shouted. 'Top priority.'

'There was a delay, then the Cam Ranh exchange operator came back on the line.

'Are you through?'

'No,' I said. 'Can you re-ring?'

'Sure.'

Another delay.

'Clarke, Manila.' the same sing-song Filipino voice answered.

'This is a call from General Joseph in Saigon,' I said, trying to sound tough, though my voice was shaking. 'Put me through immediately to Manila Commercial.'

Humming sounds emanated from the receiver. Finally, a female voice said, 'Manila Overseas, can I help you?'

'Yes, yes,' I shouted. 'Give me Sydney, Australia, please.'

'One moment please.'

An eternity passed. 'I can give you Hong Kong, but not Sydney,' the girl said.

'OK, Hong Kong will do,' I said; anything to get beyond the Philippines and into British territory.

'Hong Kong Overseas Exchange,' this time a Chinese accent answered.

'Please connect me to Sydney, Australia,' I gulped another gin and tonic while I waited. Anna was on her 10th cigarette. We were both tense.

Finally, after much clicking and fading on the line, I heard the beautiful words, 'Sydney OTC.'

'Hello, hello,' I nearly cried with relief. 'I am ringing from Saigon, Vietnam, and I was to speak to my mother on Sydney five oh nine five seven four.'

'Wha-a-a-t?' the operator said. 'Vietnam?'

'Yes, yes, hurry before the line gives out,' I begged.

She answered in typical Aussie fashion. 'Just hold your horses and I'll do all I can.'

She dialled my mother's number and I heard my mother gasp when the operator said, 'One moment, I have a call from Vietnam for you.' Poor Mother thought it was bad news.

'Hi Mum, it's me,' I shouted. She was crying with relief. It took some time before I could get her to understand what I was saying. 'Anna is coming to marry Jeff and her plane arrives in Sydney on Thursday at 8.30am, and Jeff hasn't got the phone connected at his home, so can you please drive over to his house [I gave her the address] and tell him to meet the plane and, if he's not there, will you meet Anna and look after her till she finds Jeff?'

Mother understood and repeated the message and we chatted for a few more minutes. I replaced the receiver.

'Anything is possible,' I quoted Anna, and we jumped around the trailer with joy, then had more drinks. She was committed now and had only to pack her bag and sneak off the next morning to Saigon to catch the flight to Sydney.

It wasn't a sad parting. We had become such good friends we couldn't even think that we would never meet again.

'I'll see you when you return. Look after yourself,' she said as she boarded the plane to Saigon in the early dawn light.

'Just send me the wedding photos,' I wiped away a tear impatiently, 'and thanks for the jeep.'

Then she was gone.

I drove back to the army base slowly. I had my own vehicle at last, but had lost two good buddies. 'No,' I said to myself. 'I still have two good buddies, only they're on the other side of the world. And I have a jeep too.' Things looked bright.

At the office, my civilian boss was slouching around like a bear with a sore head. He told me he had been in the middle of talking to his wife in Hawaii the previous day, when his call had been cut off for an A-1 priority call. He was very sore about it. I just smiled quietly to myself. 'Fat-cat,' I thought. 'You're not the only one with privileges, only you don't know how far-reaching mine are!'

The days went by and Christmas loomed again. I was very busy with changing over the ration and identification cards of every Third Country National in Second Corps. The C-Day money changeover had left the grand sum of $12 million outstanding and unaccounted for, and the CID and our own PX security men were frantic. They were even considering stopping all TCNs from owning or operating cheque accounts as the 'green' or 'goldflow' money was lost by people selling cheques to the Viets. I knew how this was done and had tried it only once when I was desperate for money to live on in Saigon. I had written out a personal cheque to 'cash' for $200. I had sold it to a moneychanger in Tu Do Street for the equivalent of $500 in piastres, leaving me nearly three times as much to spend on the Viet economy than if I had cashed my cheque into MPC at the finance branch, then changed it to piastres at the legal rate. My cheque was presented to my bank several months later through the Hong Kong and Shangai Bank in Hong Kong. The moneychanger had taken my cheque and whatever others he had accepted over the months and made a trip to Hong Kong, where the cheques were deposited into an account there. As all the cheques would have been from the Bank of America or the Chase Manhattan Bank (the only two banking facilities in Vietnam), there was no way that he could have been picked up in Hong Kong for exporting money from Vietnam. I still wonder how much money the communist party stashed away in its account in the Shanghai Bank that was willingly and stupidly supplied by greedy GIs and civilians in Vietnam.

It was only after the system had been explained to me and I realised where my cheque could end up and in whose hands it would undoubtedly land, that I figured I would *never* donate funds to a communist organisation under normal circumstances, and this was no different. In fact, it was worse, because I was actually supplying funds to the enemy to purchase the guns and equipment they were using daily against me. I vowed to myself to never change money illegally again, and I kept my vow.

The Bob Hope show arrived at Cam Ranh and I had front-row seats. Phyllis Diller was terrific, the leggy showgirls made the fellows all shout and swoon and Mr Hope cracked his jokes endlessly. We all stamped and shouted and yelled 'More, more' and the performers obliged. It made Christmas seem real to us.

The current Miss America was touring with Bob Hope and she was allocated Anna's old room in my trailer. She seemed to be in a daze most of the time. I figured she had never had such a reception as in Vietnam, and remembered my first reaction to the sight of hundreds of drivelling men all gazing hungrily at me. Pity that she stole my khaki bath towels though.

Ho Chi Minh had died and the Cong had been quiet since September. We were all waiting for renewed offensives and taking advantage of the calm period to celebrate with parties and fun.

The Sharkbaits had two Australian pilots living with them, learning to fly the Phantoms in wartime conditions. These two fellows, Robert and Bruce, decided that they would give an Australian-type New Year's Eve party, and had ordered Aussie wines, cheeses and other foodstuffs from Sydney for the occasion. The menu was published on the noticeboard, listing delicacies such as 'emu soup' and 'kangaroo pies'.

I rang Saigon to speak with Kerry to invite her up for the party and was informed that she had gone back to the States suddenly, as her parents had been recalled and she felt she had had enough. It had all happened fast, two days from beginning to end, and she was gone. I transferred my call to Gail, who explained that Kerry had tried to phone me, but was unable to get through because of the bad lines. She had left a letter for me and Gail would bring it up on New Year's Eve when she came to the Aussie party.

It had been a bad month at Cam Ranh. There were 350 cases of drug overdoses among the enlisted army men, which was about 10 per cent of the base. Several of the concession shops were systematically burgled and it was still quite unsafe for any female to walk unattended through the army base, day or night. I heard that one enlisted man went crazy and shot and killed his commanding officer and his non-commissioned officer, then put a bullet through his own brain. '*Three* more Purple Hearts?' I thought. I saw another GI shoot a pregnant Vietnamese in the belly, killing her and her baby. One of the PX Filipinos came to me to report the theft of three blank cheques from his quarters. He had only $900 in the bank, his savings of two years (he had been an Honest Joe). The cheques were subsequently returned through his bank, cashed at the Shanghai Bank for funds totalling $800. The poor little fellow howled on my shoulder, but what could I do? He took his $100 and went home to the Philippines.

Gail arrived for New Year's Eve and the Wing Vice-Commander, Colonel Hartcher (Norm to his friends), and I collected her at the airport. When we arrived at the Sharkbaits' mess, all ready to live it up, there was no party. The Australian ship, the *Jeparit*, on which our food and goodies had been loaded, was held up in port in Sydney owing to a communist-inspired workers' strike. We painted signs saying 'Wallop a Wharfie' and marched around the base to the various kitchens, and eventually got enough steaks together to have a barbecue instead. Twenty-three mortars landed on us that night, putting a swift end to the celebrations. Gail, Norm and I went back to Norm's large trailer and drank bloody marys until dawn, oblivious to the rockets landing around us. It was a shit of a new year, thanks to the commies both in Vietnam and in Sydney. 'A pox on them all,' was our toast that night.

The Australian Government, however, finally did right by us and commissioned the *Jeparit* into the navy. It set sail for Vietnam in early January with a full navy crew, and we received our goodies in time for an Australia Day celebration on 26 January. Gail came up again for that, but brought bad news with her from Saigon.

'All TCNs are slowly being retrenched,' she told me. 'The word around head office is that the Viet Government is getting nasty about us holding jobs that they think

Vietnamese should have, and they are really cracking down on us.'

In early March, I had a call from her to say that she was leaving. She had been retrenched.

Now I really was on my own and I knew it was just a matter of time before I was given my marching orders too.

Chapter Seventeen

THE STRAW THAT BROKE
THE CAMEL'S BACK

5 MARCH 1970

Dear Mum and Dad,

Well, today is the day that the straw broke the camel's back. I am just sick to death of American prejudice and bigotry. As you know, they divide people who work for them into groups by nationality (Number One instance of prejudice), and we Third Country Nationals at the bottom of the list are paid different salaries and living allowances for doing the same work and living on the same economy.

Last Monday, a Filipino woman who works for the PX here at Cam Ranh Bay came to the Personnel Office to see me to apply for government quarters. She is entitled to, even *authorised*, to have government billeting, the same as I am. We are United States Department of Defence *Direct-Hire employees* and, according to the military command regulations applicable to Vietnam, DOD Direct-Hire are entitled to privileges BEFORE Red Cross, USO girls, etc. We are, believe it or not, Number One on the civilian status list. But how differently this is put into practice.

Well, Mum and Dad, this girl happens to look a little different from your darling daughter and from the American girls living in the Mini Court, which is the only women's quarters on base. So the Army Command said she can't have government quarters. I asked 'How come? How come I can have quarters, but Mrs Arroyo cannot?' After all, I pointed out, there were vacancies. In my trailer was me and a black American, and a Filipina wouldn't make waves.

The answer: 'We prefer to billet our American girls first, and we are expecting some more Red Cross girls and USO girls here soon …'

I pointed out the directives authorising DOD Direct-Hire BEFORE Red Cross and USO and they pointed out that she was a 'slant-eye' (yes, they actually called her that) and not really the type of person they would want to live in such nice quarters.

Now, Mum and Dad, this girl has been paying rent for a house in Dong Ba Thin village across the bay on the mainland and lately her life has been threatened more than once by Vietcong. It is imperative to her safety that she move onto the base, and the only women's quarters are the very ones they are refusing to give her.

I cried, I was so furious about the whole thing. One American girl at the Mini Court had the gall to tell me about, 'A Hawaiian, she looks sort of Japanese, and I've asked to have her removed'. And do you know — she's getting away with it! The Hawaiian girl is being transferred.

These are the people who preach freedom, democracy, no racial prejudice (but only against blacks) — but the dreadful catch is — PREJUDICE AGAINST AMERICANS IS PREJUDICE. PREJUDICE BY AMERICANS IS NON-EXISTENT. And they really believe this.

No wonder they're losing this bloody war.

EPILOGUE

I HAD BEEN fired! There was no doubt of that. My letter of termination came from the Cam Ranh Bay Exchange Commander — not from the Saigon Headquarters.

Since the argument I had had with Major Milliner over the billeting of Mrs Arroyo on base, I had refused to attend work and had packed my gear and moved to the air base to Norm Hartcher's quarters, taking over his second bedroom. I had spent my days on the beach, swimming and sunbathing. I had spent my nights at parties or conning rides in aircraft to parties in other parts of the country where I would stay for a few days, thumbing a lift back on a flight that was going my way. I had become a Vietnam Bum, in the true sense of the word. The letter had been delivered to me by my civilian boss, who was upset and sorry that I had to leave.

So I packed my gear, collected my gambling IOUs, paid off my debts (which were few) and said my goodbyes. I never set foot on the army base again.

In Saigon, I took my passport to personnel headquarters and a little Vietnamese girl who checked it blanched visibly when she saw that there was no entry visa.

It cost me $200 to gain an exit visa from the Vietnamese authorities and it was dated 8 April 1970, and was valid for 15 days.

I counted up on my fingers. Fifteen days after the 8th was 23 April, so I booked a flight for that morning. I was determined to stay till the very last minute.

On the morning of the 23rd, I went to say goodbye to the Commander of the Vietnam Regional Exchange, Colonel Richard. He said he was surprised that I was leaving and I told him I had been fired by Major Milliner.

'He has no authority to do that, Holly,' the Colonel told me. 'If you like, I will override him and we can find you a job in another area.'

I thought about it, but only for a moment. No, things were not the same any more since my girlfriends had all left. The soldiers had lost their keenness, their sense of fun, their urgency. I figured that the US Government was scraping the bottom of the barrel for its manpower at this stage of the war, and the bottom of the barrel was not what I was used to. I thanked the Colonel and said a firm 'no'.

A depressed Carmen drove me to Tan San Nhut and waited while I changed my money into greenbacks. As I entered the cow bails and showed my passport to the Viet officer, he glanced at it, then snapped his head up and stared at me hard. I started to sweat profusely. He clapped his hands, two Viet White Mice ran forward and, at his instruction, they grabbed me and hustled me out of the terminal into a jeep. I watched the Freedom Bird take off without me, with my luggage on board, and struggled and yelled for Carmen to grab my passport.

I was taken to Precinct 512 jail, the same jail Chantou had been raped in. I was put in a cell, still shouting and yelling for the Australian Embassy. An hour later, a very harassed Carmen arrived and walked to my cell to let me out.

'Don't say a word, just let's get out of this place,' Carmen said through her teeth, and hustled me to the waiting PX vehicle outside.

On the drive back to Tan San Nhut she explained, 'You forgot to count CHINESE STYLE! Eight and 15 in this country is 22, not 23. Don't you remember, a Viet child turns two on the anniversary of his first birthday.'

'Oh,' was all I could say. I had been terrified that my illegal entry had been discovered, but apparently in all the fuss over my wrong departure date, no Viet official had checked the back pages of my passport. Perhaps my miscalculation of the date had been extremely lucky, as it had confused everybody and concentrated attention on my exit visa only.

Carmen handed me my passport, which had a red stamp over the eighth and, in handwriting above, 'I say 23 April' and a signature. She had worked hard and fast and told me I owed her $100 for the bribe she had to pay for the corrected visa. I paid her happily.

She had obtained a seat for me on the Pan Am 2.30pm flight to Bangkok and had rung through to the Thai International terminal in Bangkok for them to hold my luggage. She handed me back my 'green' money, which she had collected and counted at the jail, and as we pulled up at the airport terminal she said, 'Goodbye Holly, for the last time. This place will not be the same without you!'

'Goodbye, Miss Fix-It,' I replied, and we both burst into tears.

As we circled up in a spiral to avoid perimeter mortars, I looked down at Vietnam for the last time. I didn't know then that just a few short years later the country would fall to the communists and my beloved Saigon would be renamed Ho Chi Minh City. I did realise, though, that I could never, never come back. I broke down and sobbed.

After a while, I opened the box Carmen had given me. It contained a medal and a citation: 'The medal for Civilian Service in the Republic of Vietnam is awarded to Holly Gow for meritorious service.'

If they meant *Civilian Service* in the sense that I gave it, then I certainly earned that medal.

PANDANUS BOOKS

Pandanus Books was established in 2001 within the Research School of Pacific and Asian Studies (RSPAS) at The Australian National University. Concentrating on Asia and the Pacific, Pandanus Books embraces a variety of genres and has particular strength in the areas of biography, memoir, fiction and poetry. As a result of Pandanus' position within the Research School of Pacific and Asian Studies, the list includes high-quality scholarly texts, several of which are aimed at a general readership. Since its inception, Pandanus Books has developed into an editorially independent publishing enterprise with an imaginative list of titles and high-quality production values.

THE SULLIVAN'S CREEK SERIES

The Sullivan's Creek Series is a developing initiative of Pandanus Books. Extending the boundaries of the Pandanus Books' list, the Sullivan's Creek Series seeks to explore Australia through the work of new writers, with particular encouragement to authors from Canberra and the region. Publishing history, biography, memoir, scholarly texts, fiction and poetry, the imprint complements the Asia and Pacific focus of Pandanus Books and aims to make a lively contribution to scholarship and cultural knowledge.